The Source of the Sound

Also by Patrick Holland

The Long Road of the Junkmailer (UQP, 2006)
The Mary Smokes Boys (Transit Lounge, 2010)

The Source of the Sound

PATRICK HOLLAND

SALT

CAMBRIDGE

PUBLISHED BY SALT PUBLISHING

14a High Street, Fulbourn, Cambridge CB21 5DH United Kingdom

© Patrick Holland, 2010

The right of Patrick Holland to be identified as the editor of this work has been asserted by him in accordance with Section 77 of the Copyright, Designs and Patents Act 1988.

Printed in the UK by the MPG Books Group

Typeset in Bembo 12 / 13.5

ISBN 978 1 84471 811 5 paperback

1 3 5 7 9 8 6 4 2

for my darling Nan

Contents

Flame Bugs on the
Sixth Island

G O   D O W N   T O   the rock pools when the evening
tide is out and there is a chance you will see them.
Sometimes one will swim in among the mangroves in
the tidal flats, but the rock pools are best. Flame bugs
are what we call them. I do not know if they have other
names. I do not know where else they are found but our
island. I have never heard them spoken of by anyone
who does not live here.

The northeast wind comes in spring and blows the
flame bugs to our shores. One October in boyhood I took
to going down to the rocks alone to look for them.

I never asked the boys to come with me. I was worried
they would try to net and torment the creatures. I thought
about how the boys dragged mud crabs out from under
rocks with hooks and tried to crack their shells.

The most precious time I went looking for the flame
bugs was with the girl we called Shell. We called her
Shell as before anyone knew her she was seen collecting
shells on the south beach, and because she wore a necklace
with a by-the-wind-sailor pendant. She belonged to that
tribe of children whose European blood naturalises here;
whose blonde hair the sun and salt water turns white and
the white skin olive.

One afternoon I saw Shell sitting bored in her front

yard and, though I had planned to go alone, I asked her if she wanted to come look for flame bugs and she said that she did. We left Ooncooncoo Street at twelve-years old and six o'clock.

Shell had only recently moved to Moreton Bay: so close yet so far apart from the big city. She was lonely and a little intimidated at school. Most of us had grown up together and there were more boys than girls and we boys were very rough unless isolated. First I pitied her. Then I wondered at her: at her way of sitting with her knees beside her; at her speech and her interests that were cultivated and strange to me. I made a habit of noticing her. But I did not know how to introduce myself. This night looking for flame bugs was the first time we had truly spoken. Walking off her street I got the feeling she was excited at the prospect of making a friend, and that she would have followed me anywhere; far further than the rock pools.

She told me how at her old school she had played the violin but here there was no teacher. Her mother was doing her best in a proper teacher's stead. She told me she liked the island but for that. I told her I played a little guitar, which was true. I told her my mother, being a school teacher, could let us into the community dance hall any time we liked, where there was an assortment of old instruments and the opportunity to nurture a band, which was not true at all. Between fact and fantasy we decided her musical ambitions did not have to end. We arranged public concerts that would never take place.

We walked off the bitumen streets, through a paddock of cattle on saltwater couch, to the Esplanade lined with wooden buildings and drooping streetlights not yet lit. We came to the sand where more than a dozen tidal pools reflected the twilight arch. The sun sets quickly here and amidst the pools we stood in true twilight. I wonder if I hoped we would be left alone, or if that jealousy is mine—the man's rather than the boy's.

No one came onto the beach. The ocean was uninhabited but for a lonely fishing boat with lit mast-light in the offing.

I gave her my torch. I told her to shine it into the pools and look for the reflective eyes that would indicate the animals. You almost never found flame bugs in the tidal pools on the sand and mud and I did not hold any serious hope, only I was hoping to stretch time by putting more movements into it. A thing I knew was possible. She checked every pool on our way toward the headland where my true hope was.

We left our shoes on the sand. Our children's feet found all the footholds in the rock, and a girl of twelve gives up nothing in agility to a boy. Soon we were kneeling by a captured pool, a deep one the sea had only recently left. We did not need the torch now. Its light would not penetrate that depth of water. And anyway, all that was needed was to swirl your hand in it and if the pool held a flame bug it would light like an underwater candle.

She told me she had never seen one. If there was a flame bug here tonight I wanted it to be her find.

'You try.'

She put her arm in past her elbow and stirred the water. Two came alight.

'Ahh . . .' Her eyes shone like the bugs.

'It's a good pool,' I said. 'We're lucky.'

'Yes. We're lucky, alright.'

Though she did not know how lucky we were. It was possible to come for days on end and not see one.

'Should we look in the other pools?'

'Stay here,' I said.

'Yes,' she agreed. 'We should stay here where we've been lucky, as long as we can.'

She was beautiful then, when she spoke those transcendent words. Normally I would have gone checking the other pools and left this one that was certain. Instead I wanted to stay where she was pleased.

I told her how flame bugs were rarely seen together like this. How their eggs float on sea foam through the air. At first she did not believe me. I assured her it was true. This was what my father had told me. Perhaps he had been speculating or restating a myth, but nothing I have learnt since has falsified it. Our shores are protected—still the flame bugs seem to have no device for coping with even small waves; no muscular foot like a limpet, nor the ability or inclination to bind themselves into crevices like urchins. They are only ever seen at night. I do not know if they are resistant to high rock temperatures and drying out or if instinct tells them when evening's tides make it safe to come close to shore.

The existence of flame bugs seems to have no practical point. Nothing in the pools ever rises to snap at them. Though if they are prey to some furtive thing, their glowing when disturbed can only aid it. They cannot be eaten by humans or used for bait and they die when put in tanks. Flame bugs seem to exist only to carry light.

'Try and catch one,' I said.

'I don't want to hurt it.'

I laughed, happy in my better knowledge; happier I had the opportunity to share it.

She stirred up their lights then made a grab at one that was at the far side of the pool by the time she closed her fingers. She tried again and we laughed together.

'It's near impossible,' I said.

She sighed agreement. They could not be caught by hand.

We sat watching the flame bugs for I do not know how long. Their unpredictable movements and light meant there was no possibility of boredom. Children do not possess the accumulated pasts and over-anticipated futures that dwarf the present—happiness in the moment is complete happiness. Since time no longer pained us it was suspended.

There must have been a point that night when we decided it was late and we should return. I do not remember the decision. My parents were native islanders and did not care how late I came home, but her family was new to the island's customs and would be worried.

I did not wish it, but I found myself delivering her to her front gate. I stayed hidden behind a fig tree to see her father come out and pretend to be angry when he heard her footsteps on the path. He hugged her and took her in.

I was jealous. The night might have lasted forever had we not given up on it.

I never spent another evening with the girl we called Shell. Two years passed and circumstance and my shyness meant we never became the companions we might have. Though, if at any time during those two years I had been asked to choose one of my classmates as a favourite it would have been her. This would have surprised everyone, though not, I suspect, the girl herself.

She moved back to the city for tenth grade. The day before she left she came unexpectedly to my house. She told me she did not want to leave the island. She had not told anyone else. She took my hand. It was the second time we had been alone together. Then she left.

Three years later I heard she had been accepted into the

city conservatorium for violin. It was two years after that, having rowed back from my launch, my mother asked me if I remembered a girl who used to live on our island and pointed to a photograph in the already-old city newspaper, to a face that was hers, though I had to look twice to be certain. My mother told me the girl had been killed by a man in a nightclub who had baited her drink. She possessed a beautiful future, the paper said, that had been meaninglessly cut short. Did I remember her? I cannot explain why I lied and said I did not.

I went to the beach. I sat on a high dune and looked out at the ocean, at the riding light of a distant boat. I was heartbroken, though I had little right to be. I had not seen the girl in more than five years. I wondered if my love should stop now, as the pessimists would have it, since it became futile with the death of its object.

I looked north across a chaotic expanse of water and heard the words of the crucified thief: *remember me when you come into your kingdom.* I am frightened of God's forgetting. This clumsy attempt to write the night of her and the flame bugs is an attempt to redeem a night in time that meant something to me, in this world where not all, and ever less, of our time has meaning. I cannot be sure all I have written here is factual, though it is — in some inexplicable way — true.

I am still here on the island. I will never leave. Men still fish these waters, but they do not live on the island or build their own boats and they say there is no future in living as I do. I am not concerned with the future. I am a man who most say has done little. But I have already seen more than I understand and lost much more than I have kept.

The flame bags are few now. Like all beautiful things,

they grow fewer as the world moves degraded through time toward its end.

I walked down the beach to the headland and climbed onto the rocks. I stirred the pool, the same pool . . . An unlikely flame bug rose and lit.

I spoke to the creature, to the stars, to God. I asked them to remember the lost movements of that night that time had passed by.

Should we look in the other pools?

Stay here.

Yes. We should stay here where we've been lucky, as long as we can.

Why can't I keep you?

Deep in the pool a second bug lit and rose up beside the first like a fallen tear of light.

Integrity

God is in the midst of her, she will not be moved . . .
—PSALM 46

I TOOK MY CAR onto the Western Freeway and drove without intending any place. My marriage of two years had deteriorated to the point where the end seemed inevitable, and as one loss lay upon another in my city, which is falsely accused of resisting time, I felt there was nothing left but escape. The following examples of what I mean may seem random and eccentric . . . but a stretch of woodland I often walked at the twilight-edge of Brisbane had been turned into a brightly-lit hypermart. And on a high terrace near my home a developer had deliberately left a Queenslander to vandals in order to evade heritage listing. I first kissed my wife on the house's vine-entangled front fence. Now the house was being demolished, and the place that contained my most cherished memory was gone from the earth forever.

These and more things set me on the road.

I drove through the outskirts and suburban sprawl, that broken dream of the middle class. Cars prayed in rows to their Euclidean gods at furniture marts and office parks. Teenagers bored to violence leant against transplanted palms in car dealerships. Malignant brick estates crept over the hills. This tract could as easily be a highway in California, the outskirts of London, or the housing projects in Jerusalem as the road that becomes Highway 54.

East of the Great Dividing Range, when the sprawl releases it, the country is green and picturesque. But Highway 54 has only a brief passage there and runs its course before the famous red deserts. It crosses the country in between. Beyond an uncertain point after the Range it is traversed by road trains, town-skipping contractors and a very few bewildered tourists; these last hoping to arrive somewhere other than the unloved towns strewn along the asphalt, the unthought-of plains the towns are cast upon.

I was one of an isolated few who grew up here — if a length of road a thousand miles long can cohere, but that is how I think of it; and certainly a plain five hundred miles wide may make islands. This road is a passage into the heart of the country that occupies few imaginations. A one thousand page travel guide for Australia devotes an eighth of a page to it. The aborigines were driven out one hundred years ago. The language that grew out of the landscape's defeating distances and unremarkable marks went with them. The distance between that lost language and the amalgam of German and Latin now laid upon the country must be comparable to the distances between landmarks that cause travellers such attrition. It has been good grazing country, but it is ever less so. The salt table is rising. Summer rains are no longer dependable.

The people of the country have an understanding of it, without mysticism, but impressive in its practicality. The small number who develop a non-utilitarian affection for the land would not betray it with words like beautiful, spacious or silent. Even those who attend Church do not tolerate soft feelings, much less believe in Christ's redemption. They live in the time of Abraham, though their families are not large enough to counter what death takes away, and their nation will shortly be as obscure as the darknesses between the stars . . .

I reached the Jimbour Plain at late afternoon. Only the dim Bunya Mountains to the northeast promised anything other than flatness to any horizon. At half-past five the red sun shone directly into my eyes and I pulled the car over to let it set. I was in a town called Macalister.

I was twenty-five before I could name this town. It was just another scattering of dilapidated timber houses, a railway siding and a pair of silos. The town hugged the highway without depth, not one block back off the asphalt, as if it too felt the awful monotony that sur-rounded it and clung to the little life that dripped along the road. One house had a hopeless 'For Sale' sign pick-eted in the front yard. I remembered the sign from a year ago. A solitary motley-white tree stood in a field across the rail line to the north. The tree looked like a wind-twisted forest red gum and judging by its girth was older than all the European generations of Macalister. This year the field the tree stood in was fallow. Wired to the head post of a fence line was a weather-beaten advertisement for a soft-drink I had never heard of. An old and toothless man sat on a bench under an awning and watched the sky.

I drove across the rail line onto a rutted dirt road. I pulled over beside the field and white tree. A pair of local teenagers or passers-through-town had tried to borrow a little of the tree's permanence for their romance and scratched their initials in the trunk. The sun set and the land cooled and softened beneath a deep blue twilight. I looked northeast and took in unknown miles of grass between this dirt road and the Bunyas. I sat long enough to hear the first three odes of Pärt's *Kanon* on the car stereo and was taken by an urge to walk. I left the car and stepped through a barbed-wire fence and set out across the plain. The scattered few farm houses were a good distance away. Their lights blinked on despite the ample twilight.

I do not remember how long I walked. Suddenly I was upon the crest of a small rise. A wind picked up in the north out of the Bunyas, blowing directly across the prevailing westerly. The winds eddied in the yellow grass and lifted dull flowers and grass seed in swirling figure-eights and patterns only pencil and sketch pad could describe, like sunlit dust motes riding on thermal lifts. The wind did not release a single flower.

I stepped down an unseen bank. At my feet was verdant, flowering grass and a fan of silt and moist leaves—this in a country of fierce dry winds in rainless July. I was reminded of how even in the worst droughts the Brisbane Forest Mountains had a way of storing and rationing moisture, of protecting themselves. A light brighter than dusk was caught here and ran through the bed like water. The light seemed part of a permanent stream. I felt I could take it up in my hand. Again I was reminded of large woods and forests, the way light existed there: how it often fell down a waterway, or pierced the trees in a single suspended bar. Another step and my boots sank into mud. I stood in a narrow creek that turned blindly away to the northeast toward the Bunya Mountains and behind me to the flat west. The sound of the wind was touched by another, lower whispering: the quiet churning of a big river.

All the creeks in this country were ephemeral, and for the last year had been dry. Only a mile or so on foot from a road I had travelled more than one hundred times, I felt a stranger; and yet, never more ensconced. I sat down on the bank and ran my hand across the flowers I was losing along with the stream of light to the onset of night.

I followed the creek east in an attempt to find the river it must run to. In the dark the creek flattened out and turned away from me and the river's hushing was gone, replaced by the sound of the west wind in dry grass. I walked north for more than half a mile and discovered nothing. Looking back across the darkened plain I regretted my loss. I sought the place of mysterious light and sound I had chanced upon. I did not find it in two hours, though I knew what I was looking for this time and I knew the direction. I felt it was there, but that the night, the darkness and the strange wind-blown light of night, obscured it.

I looked west to the town. A pair of sad mercury lamps wasted their light over the bitumen. Golden lamps at the siding lit a train loaded with coal. These guided me to my car.

I drove west and arrived at my father's house at one in the morning.

My father was a stock and station agent who had travelled most outback roads between Queensland and the Northern Territory and knew almost every bit of country along them: who were the owners and the owners before that, even back to the original selections. He kept a small collection of esoteric maps in his study.

His cadastral maps went back to the mid-nineteenth century. One of south-west Queensland showed the old stock routes drovers had used right up to my youth. Between the cadastral maps, a hydrographical map from between the wars, and a recent road map of my own, I hoped to find some reference to the place I had been: the fragment of creek and its invisible river. Bewildered, indoors and at a desk with the benefit of cartography, I decided the place was near (perhaps on) a thread of stock route established in 1905 and gone out of use by 55 after a bore dried permanently and a better route was found. But no map distinguished the strange place I had walked into from the surrounding country. As I expected, no map marked as much as a dry creek within half a mile of it.

The place remembered a river that was vanished. The creek I stood in was a tributary, or thread of a braided stream, or a swale in a great meander; the little flowering shelf, an alluvial terrace.

By virtue of time and forgetting the land that was the stock route and my mysterious place had become the property of one Fergus McMahon, whose grass I had walked across and whose thousand-acre run sat both sides of the dirt road and extended a good way from there to the northeast. My father did not know the name, which meant it was insignificant. McMahon and his family had failed to make their mark.

'It's not great country anymore,' he offered as an excuse. Perhaps he thought I had made friends with one of the man's grandchildren in the city.

Strangely, the maps said the McMahon selection had never been subdivided, no part of it sold off.

My father was often given liquor to commemorate land sales and his cabinet remains stocked. I poured myself a scotch and water and leafed through a small collection of local histories. Mention of Wambo Shire and the Jimbour Plain, let alone Macalister, was scarce on my father's shelves. I thumbed through a history of Chinchilla, a cattle and produce town one hundred kilometres further west. The book was a dull catalogue of minor industrial and social accomplishments but for a page of diary entries taken from the town's oldest resident in 1940, whose girl-hood memories included the 'drunk and deranged Dixon Stapner,' who 'Squatted in a tent down on Wilkie Creek on commission to survey the land for the government . . .' who 'talked to blacks as though they were white men and eventually was killed by them.'

I took down a musty quarto on the history of Queensland surveying to 1930. The book had no index, but I found the name Stapner in its pages. Stapner was part of the Imperial Government's 'Extended Trigonometrical Survey' in the 1840s and 50s, penetrating ever deeper into the continent and opening up territory for new settlers. He was killed in 1861 on the Jondaryan Plain when a 'rival tribe ambushed his blacks'. He was called 'a superstitious man' by his peers. One mentioned the story of a stretch of country he would not enter into with his chains for reason it was 'haunted'. To exemplify the effects of drink and loneliness on inland surveyors, the volume included a page of Stapner's field book, highlighting an offset the man had made to his survey line in order to negotiate an imaginary creek . . .

There were once great waters in that country, during what the Orthodox refer to as the immeasurable day of God's rest before He blew life into the nostrils of Man. First an inland ocean — my father once uncovered a shark's tooth in the dust at a station near Dulacca — then ancient rivers that ran through forested hills.

I sat by the living room window, contemplating the mystery and listening to silence that was broken once in a while by a road train roaring along the highway. I dreamt of lonely night-time truck stops and vast distances. The cold west wind blew over the plain and in through my window making me sleep.

I returned to Macalister a day later. I drove over the railway line an hour before sunset and stood beside the singing fence line. I struck out on foot with a map bearing my own pencil marks. I walked right across the old stock route and arrived at a ruined fence bewildered. I had not set foot in the place of three nights ago. Though I was on a tremendous plain, I felt certain I would recognise it, the unusual light at least. But no part of the landscape distinguished itself. Every ten square yards seemed alike and finally dark and resistant. All that stood out in my memory of that walk were a few distant and unusually falling shadows back a way and to the north that must themselves be lost now to the coming night. Those did not seem very near to where the place must be, though now I was not sure. I turned, intending to make my way back to the road along a more northerly line and all at once I was aware of a dark and silent clamour, as loud and obtrusive as any noise or light, increasing with each step to the north. A wind rose and blew against me. The rustle of the paper map, and even the rattling of my wristwatch, seemed inordinately loud and intensified the feeling, and I knew I must go no further. I felt fear as a man would standing on the deck of a ship and imagining the inhuman depths beneath the hull — wonder and terror intertwined. I returned to my car along a south-western arc.

I drove north along the dirt road. I had the vague hope of interviewing whoever remained of the McMahons. I drove a mile and a colonial house emerged in the last flush of another flatland twilight. The house must once have been very grand. Now its white paint was all but stripped away. A pair of French doors were blown open by the wind, one falling off its hinges. A side window was broken by a branch of an overgrown mulberry tree, and all the lights were out. A couple of decades of neglect. I sighed and thought how well time does its work.

A little way down the dirt road from the house was a

timber shack. A fifty-year old body truck was in the drive. A figure crossed one of the lit windows. I pulled my car over and walked up the drive and knocked on the door. A small, bow-legged old man answered. I noticed his nose, flattened against his left cheek, perhaps kicked by a horse, and—though they say it is the last thing we notice about a person—his cold-blue eyes that reminded me of that country's dusk.

'I've run out of petrol,' I said. 'You don't have a can?'

He looked over my shoulder at the car. He said he had a drum of fuel but it was diesel. He said I should drive on another mile to Charlie Wade's place.

'I can't. I rolled this far. The car won't start.'

He asked me where I was headed.

'Nowhere. The city. I misjudged my tank, and when I got into Macalister everything was closed.'

'You should have knocked on the shop's door. Old Maggie'd sell you petrol any hour you could pay.'

I admitted it was foolish not to have done so.

The man reluctantly invited me in. He dialled 'Old Maggie'. The number was written along with half a dozen others on a three-year old calendar above the phone. He had been eating a dinner of thin stew and bread. He poured black tea from the stove and told me his name was Peter Sims.

'Not McMahon?' I said.

He told me he was custodian of the place.

'I used to work for McMahon—Fergus, and his father before him. Both dead. McMahon's boy owns the place now. He lives in the city. Doesn't take to the land.'

'Does he ever come out here?' I was thinking of the dying colonial house.

The old man shook his head.

'That boy wouldn't know this country from Mars.

Can't even saddle a horse. He pays my wages though. Same money as in his father's day.' The old man laughed. 'It yields less and less each year. I told the boy I'm too old to run it. He doesn't care. At least it's small. Not much to go to ruin.'

'A thousand acres,' I said automatically, betraying myself.

He said that was right, furrowed his brow and stared at me over his tea. We sat in a stretched moment of silence.

'I'm an old man, but I hear alright. I know what a car with a dry tank sounds like.'

I was ashamed of having lied. I forgot the old people of this country take note of the slightest event on their roads. There was no television in the house; one old and cheap transistor radio that may or may not have worked and could barely have picked up one of the bigger town's stations from out here. My car would have had his undivided attention the moment he first heard it, even a mile back. The old man probably thought I had taken him for a fool, or that I intended to rob him.

'Don't be afraid,' I said. 'I'm no thief.'

He smiled tiredly.

'What could you take from me?'

'I want to ask you about a place, on or near the old stock route, northeast of the top of this road. I'm no good in the dark, but possibly directly east of here.' And I looked out the kitchen window into the unbroken dark that signified the plains.

Sims looked up from his plate of stew and stared at me.

'It has . . . strange qualities,' I said. 'It remembers a river. I thought someone like yourself, who had worked around here, might know about it.'

He put down his spoon.

'I was a drover in this country before I was a ringer.

I only took station work after I married. My wife's been gone three years.'

He pointed to the wall, at a painted photograph of an uncommonly pretty, Jewish-looking woman — apparently much taller than her husband, with dark hair and a high-bridged nose and dark intelligent eyes. He told me they were very different people. They had come from different backgrounds. He had been hard to live with, but he had loved her very much, especially at the end, when she was not as beautiful as the photograph. I asked him her name and he said it did not matter to me and so he would not give it. I felt no offence.

'I know the place,' he said . . .

He had been tailing out cattle on the stock route in the middle of the drought of 1950, where the last of the year's feed was. There was a rise over which the cattle would not go. He told the two old black men who were under him to push them onto it. The men spoke to each other in a language he had never heard. 'Better not, Boss,' one said. Sims trusted his blacks and left it at that. But at camp that night after all were bedded he was woken by nothing more than fierce starlight and felt drawn to the place and walked into it . . .

The old man was silent. He looked out the window and saw the emptiness that I did.

I mentioned the place's absence from maps, and the McMahon land's uncommon resistance to sale and subdivision that had lasted more than one hundred years.

Sims remembered old McMahon talking about the original survey. Legend said the first surveyor had estimated distances around here on a black man's word — by how long it took to walk it.

'That place does not call everyone. That is one case, perhaps there are more, where a man feared it.'

And I recalled my irrational fear tonight.

Arthur McMahon, Sims told me, was a saturnine man, devoted to an indifferent German wife who was overcome by loneliness and returned home. After that he neither farmed the land nor let anyone onto it. He lived out his life alone in the house he built her. McMahon's Cologne born daughter never came here. She willed the land to her nephew Winchell, Fergus McMahon's father . . . In 1920 a terrible drought and deadly influenza had kept a survey party from the Jimbour Plain. In 1947 hail stones left the country looking white and snowed on and destroyed a theodolite . . .

The old man said he had walked into the mysterious place twice in his life: that night in youth and again three years ago, on the day his wife died. Then he heard surging water, pounding upon itself and overbrimming its banks, and he knew the creek's memorial river was in flood.

He told me he would not be going back there. He was going soon to where all the country was like that. There, he said, he would speak his wife's name next.

I told the old man what he knew already, that I too had been to the place, only few days ago. He nodded and said nothing. I mentioned the uncommon grass that I thought must be native, how I did not see a stem or blade of introduced pasture, not even buffel.

'Strange winds protect it,' he said.

I nodded and told him I had seen them.

'Periodic and wilful invisibility seems to be one of the place's attributes.'

But the old man shook his head. He repeated that the place was protected by winds and also by the light. The light on the plain was always changing. There were phases of the sun and moon that the landscape made no impression upon the mind and you could not recognise the place.

He looked once more out the window into the dark and returned to his plate of bland food, as if savouring something ineffable. 'All I know is it does not vanish and appear. I can feel it out there. It is the memory of God, the remnant He will use to rebuild . . . Nothing can disturb it.'

The cold wind came in through the wallboards and sucked at the glass in the window. I pulled up the collar of my jacket.

'Has a local history ever been written about Macalister or the district?'

I said I had searched but not found one.

Sims laughed and said there was no such book.

'This is not pretty country,' he admitted. 'There are few people here and nothing much happens.'

Old Maggie of the highway shop knocked once on the door and pushed it open.

'Peter!' she wailed in a condescending tone to which I saw the old man was accustomed.

I stood up from the table and greeted the robust outback woman who stood in the doorway. An unbuttoned flannel coat was wrapped loosely around her shoulders and grey wisps of hair escaped her night scarf.

She bustled me out the door before I had properly said goodbye to the old man of the shack beside the McMahon house, though I knew he would not have wanted my address or phone number, which we often exchange in the city without intending to remember a person.

Old Maggie flipped the latch of a jerry can and fastened the metal nozzle. She held the funnel while I poured. With her spare hand she held a torch. The twenty-litre can was quarter-full. I watched the lights go out in the shack.

She laughed.

'You poor bugger, stuck in there with old Sims.'

'I didn't mind.'

'Yeah. Nice old fella. Bit funny though. Keeps to himself. We look after im.'

When the can was empty we drove to Maggie's shop. She switched on a naked orange light bulb that lit the concrete and an antique bowser. A brown house moth fluttered to the light. Through the window at the back of the shop, I saw her two children sitting at the television, absorbed by some program with loud New York accents.

Maggie huddled into her coat against the cold night air. She talked about the weather that was set to go below freezing and about the television show they had been watching when I called.

'Have you seen it?'

I told her I did not own a television.

She looked at me suspiciously.

Her suspicion deepened when she realised my tank had only taken another fifteen litres of petrol.

'The gauge must be faulty,' I apologised unconvincingly.

She humphed down her nose. She followed me to the car, raised her hand abortively and stepped off the half-lit street. I drove east toward the city. A billboard collected a little stray light from the street lamps and tried in vain to impress itself upon the dark. In a motel room that night I dreamt of running water.

A Haunted Solitude

T HEY WERE BETWEEN buses in Medjugorje, coming from Trebinje to join HOS forces in Bihać in the north. Private Milo Jusufović had no interest in Medjugorje. He was in Bosnia as a solider for the Croatian people and not for any faith. Both men wore the uniform they had worn when serving with the Croatian Infantry in the defence of Dubrovnik. They came into town and a bus load of pilgrims passed them on their way north to Apparition Hill. Their own bus stopped in the centre of town and Private Jusufović saw the stalls, lit against the coming dark, selling holy paraphernalia even in wartime. An old woman inspected a row of Marian statues for chips in the plaster.

'Why don't these fools go to safety,' said Jusufović to Corporal Drago Pavić. Pavić was a Sarajevan by birth, though his parents had moved to Dubrovnik when he was a teenager. Shortly afterwards he became a professional solider. And during all of their brief acquaintance Pavić had assumed the role of instructor to the young private on the state of the war and the country. He had been sneering at the woman buying statues and staring at his hare-lip in the reflective window when Jusufović questioned him.

'Because they're just that,' he said. 'Fools. They think nothing can touch Medjugorje. Ask them! You're not a believer are you?'

'No.'

'How could a man be? How could a man be after this?'

He waved his finger in the air to indicate all the appalling events of the war.

'*They* claim her too, of course. She's part of their devotion. It's a point of wounded pride that she would appear here in Herzegovina and not Serbia. So you think this place won't get hit? Anyway, the visionaries said she had blue eyes, like a pretty Croatian girl. Maria was Palestinian. How would she have blue eyes?' Pavić laughed. 'We're all alone in this world. You can be sure of that.'

They got off the bus and the old woman from the stall brushed past them with the statues she had selected. The vendor grabbed Jusufović by the arm.

'All blessed by a priest,' she said, and Jusufović saw that it was not only Marian statues she sold, but rosaries, medals, and painted postcards of the town's child visionaries.

Pavić smiled and took out his revolver.

'This was blessed by a priest in Dubrovnik. And the shells they're firing into Sarajevo are blessed by priests in Belgrade. This whole war is blessed by priests.'

Jusufović had one of the postcards in his hand. Pavić pointed to a dark-haired teenage girl.

'This one was very beautiful when she was young. Shame she's so religious. I wonder if she's in town?' He laughed and lit a cigarette. 'This old crow would probably sell us a girl if we asked.'

Jusufović smiled and went a little red in the face.

'You want to ask?' said Pavić.

'No,' the younger man smiled, and it was clear that he did want to.

Pavić pinched his cheek and turned to the vendor.

'My friend and I are between buses. We are lonely. We are soldiers for the Croatian people and very lonely.'

The woman understood and directed them without another word.

They walked down an alley in the Bijakovići district, not far from the church, to a traditional wooden house that bore no sign of its current use.

'There are no girls,' said the woman who had to be called from dinner. She was not made-up like the kind of Madam Jusufović had seen in Italian movies in Dubrovnik. She looked like someone's mother, a salesman's tired wife.

'It's only half-past eight,' said Pavić.

'I don't care if it's three in the afternoon. I've got no girls for you. I only have two on any day. One is out working. The other is sick.'

'Then we'll wait for the healthy one to come back. After all, how long can a priest screw?'

The woman laughed.

'There are other trades in this town. The girl is with a commanding officer.'

'Ah. A general? Is it Petković? I heard he was on leave down here. The old swine.'

The middle-aged woman smiled.

'A boy soldier, and talking as though you knew Petković! Anyway, it's not Petković, and there's no point waiting. The client will keep the girl all night. It is his custom.'

Pavić slapped Jusufović on the back.

'And they call this town blessed.' He turned back to the woman. 'How sick is the sick girl? I don't mind a day or two in the infirmary.'

The woman sighed.

'It's Friday isn't it?'

'Yes, it's Friday,' said Pavić, a little mystified.

'Then she has sickness unto death.'

'Can we catch it?'

The woman chuckled.

'I don't think so. I can sell you a beer each; or coffee and some cheese. That's all.'

'Let's go,' said Jusufović standing up. 'After all, the girl's sick.'

'She's not sick,' said Pavić, having decided it was the curse of Eve. He pulled the emblem on his shoulder. He leant across the desk. 'Listen, woman. Me and the boy here have been wounded already on our home soil. I'm missing three toes in one boot and young Milo here got shot in the back. It's a miracle he's alive. Now we're going to Bihać to keep the Serb pigs from places just like your town, and we'll probably die doing it. If we fail, in a month's time you'll be giving your girls to Serb soldiers and if you're lucky by way of payment they might not to shoot you.'

'Watch your mouth,' said the woman, but both men saw she had weakened.

Pavić snatched Jusufović's wallet and put one hundred convertible marks on the table.

The woman stared at the money. She flicked a switch on the wall that lit the second storey and led the men up the stairs and knocked on a door.

'Zofia!' she called. 'Are you clothed?'

A faint cry of yes came back.

'I've turned the electricity on in your room.'

'But why,' came the small voice behind the door.

The woman turned to the men.

'One at a time. And if either of you tries anything funny, if she gets hurt, you'll have a more serious man than Petković to answer to. You hear me?'

'Yes, madam,' Pavić answered.

The woman opened the door and revealed a little

gypsy girl, no more than sixteen. The girl got to her feet
in a corner of the room enshrined with icon cards of Mary
and the saints. But for a single candle on a stool where
she had been kneeling, the room was unlit. The gypsy girl
gasped with horror.

'No, Mirna. It's Friday!'

The woman sighed. 'Just this once, my dear. These are
good boys. They won't hurt you.'

'But I am hurting.'

The woman became stern.

'Listen, Zofia. Haven't I sympathized with this?
Haven't I done everything I can to please you, night after
night such as this, so many times I don't know. Tonight
you can do something for me and for your country. These
boys are going to war.'

'I don't have a country,' said the gypsy girl.

'So be it. Then do it for my sake. There's a war on
and it concerns all of us. It costs me money to keep you,
you know!' The woman was angry now. 'This time you
obey.'

And she left down the stairwell.

Pavić turned to Jusufović.

'It's only fair that you go first. After all, you paid.'

Jusufović shut the door behind him. He sat down
on the bed, unsure what to do. He had never taken a
whore before. The gypsy girl stood unmoved, watching
him with a look of veiled pain. He thought she was very
beautiful. Her dark, greasy hair hung loose over her darker
eyes. Her thin body and swollen hips showed through her
white dress in the candlelight.

'Are you really sick?' asked Jusufović.

The girl nodded silently.

'For God's sake don't look at me like that,' Jusufović
sighed. 'Just tell me — can we do it or not?'

'Tomorrow,' the girl said in the accent that could sound so harsh in men and old women, but seemed exotic and beautiful to Jusufović in the mouth of a young girl.

Jusufović stood and put his hands on her shoulders.

'I won't be here tomorrow. I'm leaving in a few hours. Before the sun. You'll think I'm an idiot for saying this, but I think I'm already in love with you.' And, being only a boy, watery-eyed tired and encountering feminine softness on the brink of hardships that had begun to take shape tonight, he believed he spoke perfect truth. In his mind he saw her before the war, before she worked at this house, wrapped in a woollen shawl with a mongrel dog at her heel, the wild, dirty hair of gypsy children blowing across her eyes . . . Now he was in the east, alright. It had nothing to do with crossing borders so much as sitting beside this girl in the pseudo-pansion. He imagined a gypsy man with ashen beard who was her father, playing a violin by the road with his family under an umbrella in a mule-drawn cart . . .

The candle guttered and went out. A distant street lamp offered hazy, insufficient yellow light. Jusufović found the light switch but it did not work.

'The woman said she turned it on.'

'The electricity rarely works.' The gypsy girl put the back of her hand on the cold bars of an oil heater to confirm this.

The girl winced and sucked her teeth and fell with some mysterious pain and Jusufović caught her.

'I can't,' the girl whimpered. And she held out her hands. Jusufović's innocence made her divulge her secret to him. She lowered her eyes. 'I have invisible stigmata.'

'What?'

'The wounds of Christ. I feel them, though they don't manifest.'

'You feel them now?'

The girl nodded.

'I've had them since I was thirteen. They can come at any time, even when I'm sitting reading, or out for a walk, but always on Friday. They're worst at three o'clock. On Easter Friday they're so bad I can hardly bear it.'

'Where do you feel . . . the pains?'

'In my hands and feet—but not my side. I don't know why. St Catherine of Sienna had it. Many . . . saints. Though, of course, I'm not a saint.'

She brought a book of saints' lives from under her bed as proof. She had bought the book with money she made here at night.

Pavić heard snatches of the quiet conversation and knocked on the door and then shouted through it.

'Doesn't sound like there's much screwing going on in there. Remember we've got a bus to catch.'

'Leave us alone,' said Jusufović.

He heard Pavić curse and step away from the door and walk downstairs. Then the front door opened and closed.

'You see, I can't today,' said the girl. 'Not while the pain lasts. How could I? It would be sacrilege.'

So this girl too, he thought, had succumbed to the collective hysteria of Medjugorje.

'If you're religious, what on earth are you doing here?'

'I wanted to paint plaster saints, but the priests wouldn't hire me.'

She did not know who killed her parents. Maybe the Serbs, or reactionary Croats, or perhaps it was an American missile . . . Only one day her mother and father and all her aunts and uncles were dead. She lived with her brother in a tent in a cemetery for a time. Then her brother disappeared, likely he was killed by militia. She had no family and no one to help her. She had heard of the mysterious appearances of the Mother of God in Medjugorje. She stole enough money for a bus ticket and prayed for forgiveness. But here there were no jobs. A whore was all the war allowed her to be.

'I've been luckier than most girls. Many of my people end up at slave markets on the borders. The woman here is mostly kind to me.'

Jusufović was shocked. Slaves belonged to the time of the Old Testament. Surely the girl was lying. Surely there were no slave markets in a place so close to his home.

She had never been baptized. Baptisms were mentioned in her book of saints, but she thought the sacrament was something only the saintly received by election. It never occurred to her to go to a church and ask for it. She said she was saving up for a bible. She might have bought a bible instead of the book of saints, but the latter was easier to read and had beautiful icon plates. Jusufović asked if she went to Mass. Not often. The wives of the city would not drink from the cup after she had taken communion. She supposed they did not bear her any ill will, merely that they were frightened of disease. But few of the men and girls and only one old woman took Christ's cup once her lips had touched it, so she preferred to go alone in the day to pray when no one was around.

'You're Catholic, aren't you?'

It had been ten years since Jusufović prayed, as a boy under his mother's orders; the same number of years since he had been in a church.

'I'm Croatian, I was born in Dubrovnik. So yes, I suppose. Though—'

'I knew it,' the girl said. 'So you understand?'

The gypsy girl winced and cried a little and fell again into Jusufović's arms.

'Are you alright?'

'I suffer at night.'

Jusufović thought that what the girl suffered from most was lack of decent food. Though her hips were wide they were all bone. Her waist seemed no wider than a tank's gun barrel.

She sat up and pulled the hood of her coat over her dark hair and looked out the window where snow had begun to fall. Jusufović looked at the dead stove in the corner behind the girl's guttered candle. He cleaned the hearth and lit a little unburnt timber with his knife and flint then came back to the bed and held her hand. He did not care if she was crazy. They sat in a period of blissful silence. He locked his fingers around hers. He did not know where Pavić had gone, but he could not hear him downstairs anymore, even after a half-hour and then an hour had passed: an hour of holding a gypsy girl's hand and watching snow fall past a solitary yellow streetlight into the dark. Then unmeasured time asleep.

At last Pavić came stomping up the stairs. He knocked once and opened the door. He had gotten into a fight with a Bosniak from the Patriotic League who was also between buses. That and a round of cards and whisky at a late-open café were what delayed him.

'My turn.'

The girl clung to Jusufović and shook her head. The young man shook her off, sat up from the bed and smoothed his uniform.

'Leave her,' he said. 'She doesn't want to.'

'Doesn't want to?'

'She's sick. It's my money we paid with. Just leave her. Go into town. Here!' He took out his wallet and gave Pavić twenty marks. 'Go get a drink.'

Pavić saw the girl shudder and thought it was his harelip that frightened her.

'I've had a drink. I'll get another just as soon as I'm done.'

The girl clung to Jusufović's arm.

'Leave her. She has . . . God won't let her do it tonight. Just leave her.'

'God?' Pavić laughed. 'So even the whores in this town are holy! Listen, gypsy, if God had anything to do with it you wouldn't be a working in a place like this. But you are. And we are soldiers. There has always been a pact between our tribes: whores and soldiers. So honour it.'

'I can't,' the girl whimpered.

Pavić was not laughing anymore. He felt tired and offended and venomous. He pushed Jusufović aside and threw the girl into the corner of the room by her hair.

'You can't hurt me,' she said, and she held up her hands as proof, though Pavić could not understand. 'While God is here there is nothing you can do to harm me.'

Jusufović did not know if it was pain or fear that showed in her face.

'Where is God?' said Pavić.

'On the Cross,' she cried. 'I feel it. He's dying at your hands.'

'My hands? Unless God was a soldier in the JNA or one of a pair of old Serb vigilantes I shot in woods near Mostar, then I had nothing to do with his death. Nothing can hurt you? You're talking to a man who's seen a boy's body ripped in half by bullets while he was praying. Nothing is going to protect you, girl. You're all alone.' Pavić began undoing his belt. 'It's such a small thing to do,' he said. 'And I'll be gentle as a lamb.'

Jusufović caught his shoulder. Pavić pushed him aside.

'Get your hand off me, boy.'

Then Jusufović took his pistol from the floor and pressed the barrel against Pavić's head.

'Leave her.'

'You filthy son of a Serb slut. Put that thing away!'

Jusufović pulled back the hammer and his finger shook in the trigger housing.

'Leave her.'

In a few minutes they were standing outside in the cold.

'I'll have you arrested,' said Pavić on the way to the bus station. 'Pulling a weapon on a superior! You'll be lucky if you're not shot.'

But as yet they belonged to no real army and there was nothing Pavić could do. The awful thing was that Jusufović was not sure he would not have pulled the trigger had it come to it. He did not answer Pavić. He had said nothing since they left the brothel.

'Apologise this instant, you bastard. I demand it.'

Jusufović looked in Pavić's eyes that were the eyes of a spoilt child. Pavić might well pull a pistol on him here and now; shoot him and drag him into an alley. Jusufović was not sorry for what he had done. Yet he said he was.

'You should be too, you whore-loving, God-loving dog.' Pavić pointed over his shoulder. 'You see that hotel there — the pink one with the Dutch trimmings? It has one hundred rooms. The Virgin Mary authorized it — so said one of the visionaries. The Dutch owner is making a packet, even in wartime. Our Lady has a good nose for business,' Pavić snarled. 'You idiot.'

They waited in silence for the bus. The moonlight and a few streetlights lit the wet pavement and the rows of stalls that were bolted down now. Tomorrow the locals would begin the trade in holy souvenirs afresh.

Outside the city centre there were hardly any lights. A few lonely guards burnt wood and old tyres in drums at the edge of town. The bus ran alongside the Neretva River and Jusufović could see the emerald-green water glinting in the moonlight. Then they rolled through the karst. Then ancient woods wrapped in darkness. He guessed only Bosnian wolves and a few hardy hunters and woodsmen survived in those.

Looking into the dark he thought what a lonely place the world was. To keep his loneliness at bay he thought of the girl forced into a corner in tears, defending her wounds. He truly believed he loved her.

The Passenger

It is the highway that drives . . . we are passengers
—Liu An

I AM IN A CAR travelling into the night. Once I believed I was driving home, but I hardly trouble with that hope now, it disturbs my peace. I think I was part of the five o'clock rush. I remember a city where I set out, though I do not recall its name. I suppose I could try to find it in an atlas the next time I stop for fuel. Though likely my next stop will be at a sand-drift, where I will step out of the car and look up and down the road as though I were not upon this predestined highway but a tourist who has lost his map, with a thousand choices unto error or home.

In the beginning I, we, (in cities one seems to be always sharing isolation with untold others) . . . I crawled excruciatingly past the backs of Chinese restaurants, monotonous apartments, twinkling car dealerships and deserted train stations. I pitied the vagabonds who roamed those dusky haunts in search of dropped coins and half-smoked cigarettes.

One day such as this, I thought, when I am more able, less tired, I will pull off the road and make a home for a night with one of them, and a meal, so he will know kindness, if only once in his life . . . but the traffic pushed me on. 'One day, old father,' I said to a ragged man who sank against the wall of a stationmaster's office.

The empty train platforms gave way to angular hypermarts, then steel yards and brickworks. I sighed when I crossed a disused rail line and saw a pair of South-East Asian prostitutes put out cigarettes with their shoes and disappear inside a concrete brothel, then a pair of bored aboriginal children spilling each other's blood in a car park. But the highway soon relieved itself of people. In the twilight I drove past abattoirs and iron sulphite smelters where all that moved was machinery and electric lights.

Each time I stopped for coffee and a cigarette at a service station the number in the cafeteria was fewer and more silent. Every town was bypassed — a mere scattering of indistinguishable lights, just far enough off the highway to make no sense of. Instead of towns, commuter villages divided the industrial outskirts that frayed into open plains. The bright lights of the dashboard meant I saw the landscape through my own dim reflection. My face hovered in the stars like a god. Miles of plain passed between my left eye and my right. Then the plains gave way to more outskirts, and I did not ever come to a place I could identify, a place I remembered.

I stopped at a roadwork. On the embankment between silos and empty rail cars an auburn-haired girl sat huddled in a duffel coat. I wondered what she was waiting for out here so late at a forgotten siding. But when she lifted her face to the orange road lamp I saw it was the face of an angel. Her hair that was the colour of the lamplight hung dishevelled about her pale, resplendent face and her wet blue eyes met mine. (How did I know her eyes were blue at such a distance, eight-feet at least? And through a window! But I am sure they were the most startling sapphire.) Our eyes joined in a communion of unknowable sadness. I knew in that instant that I loved her. Our gaze remained unbroken until the makeshift traffic light turned green and my rear-view mirror caught a road train's headlights and I was forced to drive on.

I watched the girl's dimming face over my shoulder like listening to a bell, never certain when the sound has finished and you are only hearing memory. When reason told me her face must surely be gone, I returned to the dark plains.

I thought of nothing but the girl for hours after. She occupies my thoughts even now, as you see, and I must call it love; my memory contains no stronger attachment to give that name to. As an act of fidelity I made up my mind never to look at another woman should she appear on the wayside, however beautiful. Perhaps, measured against the great loves . . . I have forgotten the names of their enactors . . . but those in Dante and Homer and Shakespeare . . . Troilus and Beatrice: were they a pair? . . . against those ours might be a petty infatuation, yet I think I would die a thousand deaths upon ancient battlefields for my girl of the railway siding if the universe had provided those. But I am only a commuting insurance salesman, and I have only this car, this highway, and a landscape that is ever emptying.

I drove through long tracts of suburban wasteland: empty concrete houses below networks of electrical pylons. The beautiful rows of lamps curving out to the horizon meant more highway, the outskirts that belonged to no city: airports, oil refineries, factories, gas fields . . . These appeared then disappeared. Then even industrial tracts became rare. I began wondering how far I had come. I had some notion when the highway stopped for a sand-drift.

After uncounted hours of driving I pulled into a brightly lit desert roadhouse to refuel. Only one old woman sat in the cafeteria. I bought coffee and a ham sandwich and sat down at a table. The light inside was so bright I could not look out. I watched my reflection in the wide glass windows. I saw how tired I had become. There was a national chain motel beside the roadhouse, but my tiredness had passed beyond sleep.

Perhaps a half hour had passed when a man, two or three days unshaven and wearing a filthy flannel shirt, sat down in the seat across from me. I saw then that the window was not completely blind. It admitted the lights of a row of pumpjack rigs in an oil field, and the rigs seemed to peck at the man's head like a flock of awful metal birds.

'You must say you know me?' he whispered.

'Excuse me?'

'Pretend we're old friends.'

I noticed a leather rucksack squeezed between the man's knees and realised he had no intention of sitting it on the floor as any normal person would have. I think he caught me glancing at the bag and he closed his hand tight around the straps.

'We'll have to get a story together,' he said. 'Where are you headed? Say we're both headed there—that I'm your cousin and I'm travelling with you. I'm Gordon Williams. Which one's your car?' He squinted hopelessly at our reflections.

I asked the man to explain himself. He assured me he was an honest man wronged. At least, he said, his sins were no greater than any other man's, only circumstance had been unkind to him.

'Every human being that isn't a milk-blooded coward has a lawbreaker inside of him,' the man declared, 'only some never get the chance to reveal it. Then there's others who find nothin else.'

I asked him where his own car was. I was shocked to discover he had walked the highway to here. The radio tells us no suspicion of highway walkers can be too great. The walkers do not live in proper houses and cities but in the Anecumene. Beyond the lights. Thieves and murders dwell amongst their scattered number. So we are told. Often I wonder. But so we are told. I told the man I'd be happy to help him in any way I could, only I would not lie.

'No good end can come from lying.'

'Good will come from it this time,' the man pleaded. Then he winced horribly. 'At least let me sit with you. Just nod your head if anyone asks you to confirm what I say.'

'You can sit where you like, but I can't promise anything else.'

In fact, I believe I would have done what he asked had it come to that. I think frequently of my lost friend now he is gone. Was I pious, unkind? He must have seen the anxiety in my face, my determination to remain undisturbed, and did not trust it. When next I returned to my coffee the man I knew as Gordon Williams leapt up. He ran out of the brightly-lit roadhouse into the freezing desert night, as homeless and desperate as any creature could be. I went to the window and watched his vague outline disappear into the spinifex. Would he find his way by the highway lamps? Or did he understand the emptiness out there? I hoped he had a coat in that bag of his. I wondered if, after all, that was all he carried there, a few personals: a change of clothes, a book to keep him company. Why had I denied him? Then I reassured myself I hadn't, it was only a misunderstanding. I took my hand from the glass pane that betrayed the chill outside and repeated the assurance to myself.

I walked outside to smoke and found my car gone. Stolen. By the man who had just left me? . . . but I had seen him run into the desert . . . Perhaps some other highway rogue.

I complained to a helpless cafeteria waitress. She told me she would phone the police. Otherwise I could hire a car from a satellite about an hour, or maybe two, down the road. A bus would take me that far. The bus stopped here in three-quarters of an hour. I asked what city the satellite belonged to. The waitress looked at me with bemusement.

'Would you like me to phone the police?'

'No, thank you. I'll take the bus.'

'I'll phone them anyway.'

'Please don't.'

For all I knew the highway patrol had seen me sitting with Gordon Williams and it was they who had confiscated my car to search it, to trap me! Out the corner of my eye I saw the waitress dial a number and speak brief words that I could not make out. I stood at the door and looked across the concrete and bowsers and down the lamp-lit highway, on watch for I knew not what, as though the man whom I must call Gordon Williams had left his guilt in the roadhouse and it had attached itself to me. I even searched the cafeteria for that bag of his, though I was sure I had seen him carry it off.

I do not know what I would have done had I found the bag: would I have left it where it sat, to torment me, acting surprised when the authorities discovered it, and me the only man left in the cafeteria? I tried not to envision myself on my knees imploring that faceless authority to take into account the kind of peace-loving man I was, spewing the truth—so far as I knew it—like a frightened child at his feet, the truth of the man I did not know, the truth that sounded more brittle than any lie and made me a scoundrel. Or would I take the bag out the doors, cross the highway and throw it into the desert, thus risk giving rise to a list of questions I could not answer without appearing guilty?

But there was nothing in this roadhouse cafeteria to incriminate me—except the old woman. I had almost forgotten about her, all but hidden at a table in the back corner. She must have heard everything, the whole conversation with Gordon Williams, and she had seen me searching nervously for something I did not find under the tables. She might testify, falsely but factually, that I had some relationship with the outlaw Gordon Williams. Should I drag her out into the desert as I would have done the bag? No, my non-existent reader, do not turn from me. This is not a narrative of madness—what an awful inconvenience madness would be. I dismissed the violent thought the minute it came. Though the old woman's testimony sent me to prison, I would not be a murderer. Yet these thoughts do come to we who are basically good; they come so coldly and gently they barely unhinge a nerve, and we, thank goodness, dismiss them with equally cold reason.

I began to question the intent of my journey. Had I really set out with the intent of getting home, or was I, like Gordon Williams, running from some terrible sin? I tried to recount my ten years of life in the city . . . sins a plenty, one or two I would never admit to anyone . . . but these, like the lines of an optical illusion, seemed to refer to some central other that memory could not quite bring into focus.

When an official-looking man came through the front

door I had all but resigned myself to my fate. He bought a coffee and sat down at the table next to me. I was sure he was an undercover policeman. I stared straight at my reflection in the window. The man asked where I was going. Then, if I felt lonely on such a long trip. I said I did not. I think I gave no hint of any relationship with Gordon Williams. The man seemed to tire of me and went and sat down near the old woman's table. The pair spoke, then the man left without questioning me again and I sighed with relief.

In time I stood in the cold at the edge of the highway, waiting for the bus with the old woman. When we boarded we doubled the number of passengers.

The bus stopped shortly down the road at a research station where the Milky Way littered the sky and made the desert speciously beautiful.

Having escaped the authorities I felt elated. I devised a little joke, a fantasy. I told the old woman my name was Gordon Williams. Out here alone with a stranger on the highway, a lie over something as inconsequential and unprovable as a name seemed no different to the truth. I told the old woman I was on the run. She asked me from whom and for what, and I said it was best that she did not know.

'You won't grass will you?' I used the verb I would never use, that sounded slick to me but is probably already out of fashion.

'Who would I tell?' and she looked up at the stars as if to illustrate the distance we were from anyone and everything.

The conversation fell flat. I felt foolish for having lied. Somehow the old woman had seen through me, and I knew I had lost her as a travelling companion. She got off at the next stop and my lie was gone with her. I was glad. Now there would be no more uneasy silence between us.

The land out the window became so monotonous that the only way to measure time was by the succession of my thoughts. I fell asleep watching the obscure shapes of the desert play over my face, the rise and fall of power lines.

A slice of time was divided by the appearance of a child. She stumbled to my seat, eyes red and swollen with tears. I asked what was wrong. She told me she had lost her father.

'And your mother?'

She shook her head silently, and I supposed she was lost too.

'They must be on the bus,' I assured her. 'They cannot have gotten off and forgotten you.'

I stood up and took the girl's hand, but she shook her golden, dishevelled head.

True, we were the only people in the coach. I sat down again.

'You must have lost them at a stop. We'll phone at the next one, whenever that comes. No doubt your parents will be out on the road fretting, phoning the bus company as we speak.'

The girl's bottom lip stopped quivering and she rubbed the last of that highway of dirty tears from her eyes and sat down beside me.

How could anyone lose such a creature? I thought. A whole life could be turned to the care of such a one. I looked at her reddened face. Her eyes stared out the window, even at that awful landscape, with childish wonder. I felt happier than I had all night. And I thought how reluctantly I would part with the girl. I hoped the bus would not stop in the longest time. I imagined her father must be only a stop or two away, would probably have overtaken the bus in a hire car and at the next opportunity would board the coach to reclaim her. I dreamt of arguing with that careless man. If the girl were mine I would never have left her alone to get lost and go crying to strangers, some of whom might even be dangerous! Out here was so far from everything, and loneliness could easily become a sense of impunity.

The girl closed her eyes, closed her hands around my hand and leant on my shoulder. I sighed and looked out the window at the dark. I saw the reflection of the sleepy little girl in the window pane and I recognised the features of the auburn-haired girl of so long ago: the girl of the outskirts railway siding whom I loved. The one beside me might have been her younger sister, or her daughter. I stroked her head and smiled and watched her sleeping face glide over desert dunes, and I joined my child in sleep.

Was it a dream? But when my eyes half-opened out of sleep it was not a desert of sand I saw outside the coach but one of water, as though the asphalt ran along the surface of a great black ocean.

I woke and realised the comforting weight on my shoulder was gone. I stood up and called—not the name I did not know, but merely 'child'. There was no answer, and the window showed me sand dunes once more.

I rushed up and down the aisle, hoping against fear to find her curled in one of the seats. But she was nowhere. Had the bus made a stop, found a station while I slept? Perhaps she had found those careless guardians of hers there; perhaps the father had crept into the coach and taken her from me by stealth; or perhaps she had stepped off the bus and gotten lost. At the next stop I would speak to the driver. I would telephone . . . someone. It might be that we would have to report the lost girl to the police of whatever agonisingly large district we were now travelling through . . . I sighed and fell back into my seat and pressed my forehead against the window.

At the next stop I did none of those things, imagining my despair at the end of them, the crippling despair at having tried and failed to secure my happiness. Better to imagine it was about to walk back to my seat as miraculously as it had before. One stop came, then another. At the third I did not feel the ache in my heart so acutely.

The bus driver pulled into a highway village for the night. I gave my card number to an all night rental company in exchange for a vehicle . . .

Now the landscape flattens into an ashen desolation. The belting wind makes it hard to hold the car on the road. I pay the fuel bowsers with my card. I see no one. The radio picks up nothing but static, else strange signals I can make nothing of, but I do not believe they are meant to be music . . . If the landscape sent me a single embittered tree, or a farmhouse light however distant, it would divide my time into compartments: before, during and after . . . but all that remains are my memories, growing as informal as the desert outside, as unimpressive as the constant guttural rush of wheels on the road, whose constancy, at least, is a comfort, a form of sleep . . .

The Sons of Cain

*. . .and possible still to perceive Her a little in the dazzling
light of the great Darkness?*
—Léon Bloy, 'She Who Weeps'

B ROTHER LUCIO HAD been stonemason at the *Mon-
astero di San Giovanni Terra Furoris,* but he no longer
practised that or any other art. Instead, he devoted his
life to pilgrimage. He had returned only this day from a
year's journey to the holy places of Iberia. He had walked
the Way of Saint James through the Pyrenees to *Santiago
de Compostela* and down to Toledo for the expiation of
sins. In a library in Toledo he had translated two short
and unsolicited books for the monastery's library: verse
by a Navarrene mystic and a volume of North African
travellers' tales, whose first scripted pages he and a young
illuminator called Antonio viewed now in the fading
southern light.

'Extraordinary accounts,' said Brother Antonio.

'Their validity I cannot always attest to,' Brother Lucio
smiled. 'An account by an English monk tells of a desert
inhabited by devils that lead men by song, deep into the
dunes, to perish.'

'You don't believe in devils?'

'I have seen knights storm a sleeping village under a
Golden Bull; I have seen a man hung in a German street
for the theft of a chicken. Devil's are among us, Antonio.

But I have been in a desert, and it was not without benevolence. There were secret waters. At night the stars reached down and made you welcome. And desert winds often sound like song.'

'I envy you your travels, Brother.'

Brother Lucio tilted his head and raised his eyebrows.

'A monk without his cell—'

'Yes, I know what is said.'

Their attention was drawn to the sunset, reddened tonight by the smoke of fires in the wooded valley below the monastery.

'The villagers celebrate a birth,' said Antonio.

Women's voices rose up to the window carrying song. Likely, the father of the newborn was not present. Most of the young men of the village had left to find work in the malaria-infected marshes to the north.

Brother Lucio turned quickly from the window. He put his hand in the deep pocket of his habit and withdrew a bar of sun-hearted vermilion and another of lapis lazuli.

'I wanted to bring you ultramarine, but none was pure.'

'No matter, Brother.' Antonio lit a candle and held the lazuli to the light. 'I have my own method of grinding. A travelling monk taught me in your absence. These are wonderful, Lucio. I already see their use: illuminations for my *Gospel of Saint Luke*.'

'For the library or a church?'

'Neither,' the young man sighed. 'For a noble of Cosenza.' Then the light came back into his face. 'I'm making a triptych: Annunciation, Nativity and *Stabat Mater Dolorosa*. Tomorrow the first picture will be finished. But now I will begin some miniatures for your African Tales.'

'By candlelight?'

'Yes.'

'You do not find it false?'

'Squint your eyes and candlelight turns into the Cross. That cannot be chance.'

'I also liked the candle-lit hours best at your age.'

'And now?'

Brother Lucio translated the light he had come to know on the roads into the canonical hours.

'Before Terce and after, and the hour before Nones. The light that is bright and constant.'

'Then come to the scriptorium before Nones tomorrow and I will show you my Annunciation.'

Brother Lucio rose.

'You will not come to the meal?' he asked.

'I am fasting. My passions run too high these days. Hunger tempers them.'

The next day after Prime, Brother Lucio occupied himself with Father Benizi in the monastery gardens.

'You visited her mother,' said Benizi.

Two years ago the old priest had heard Lucio's confession.

'Yes.'

'She is—?'

'As well as can be expected. By the Grace of God she copes.'

'That is good.'

'Yes,' said Brother Lucio. 'That is good.'

'The girl's death, and the child's, they must have been . . . in some way not given us to understand . . . God's will.'

Brother Lucio nodded and looked across the land to where cliffs fell away to the ocean. The ocean was filled with gentle light. He looked back over his shoulder to the far-away that belonged to her.

'I wish they had lived.'

Father Benizi nodded. 'Yes. Of course.' And he returned to harvesting his artichokes.

Lucio sighed and echoed the words he spoke in the confessional two years ago: 'She was so young, Father. I would have left the order and married her. But now . . . So many things I should have done . . . Brought a better physician. Given her my blood. I wanted to but—'

'You were in that country quarrying stone. You could not have known what was best to do.'

Benizi put a large artichoke in Lucio's hands and smiled gently. Brother Lucio thought how he might like to settle himself into some work here at the monastery: not carving stone, but here in the gardens, even construction work in the village. There was talk of a village infirmary. The mule track to the monastery was often washed out by rain and lay under thick snow in winter and was an added sufferance for the sick.

When the yellow sunlight turned white Lucio remembered Brother Antonio and went to the scriptorium.

'It is full of air,' said Lucio, scanning Antonio's Annunciation. 'As though I could walk into it.'

The light in the picture fell true to life. But for the burnished-leaf halos crowning the central figures there was no gold. The tones brought to mind the woods around San Giovanni's; the figures, the charcoal sketches Antonio had made of peasant women and shepherds as an oblate.

'There is more of earth here than heaven, Antonio.'

'The two may meet. You have seen the northern cathedrals.'

'From where did you take it?'

Antonio beamed and tapped his head then pointed out the window.

'Up here, and out there! The event took place on earth, Brother. Too many artists have the Virgin living in a lofty palace. Giving birth in a manger of golden hay.'

'Only to signify glory.'

'A waste. Hay and wood are already more glorious than gold. Try to feed an ox gold filings. A golden world is a dead world.'

Lucio returned to the picture. He furrowed his brow when he took in Saint Joseph's turned back in the distance. Then he fixed on the central figure. At first glance he had perceived only a vague strangeness about the girl Maria, now he saw where the strangeness came from and was startled. Thin like a half-starved peasant, skin impure with red splotches and even dirt; she could be a shepherdess of Calabria. There was nothing serene about her. Her face was turned not toward but away from the Angel Gabriel with an expression of fear. Not only fear, Brother Lucio realised—distaste.

'What do you say, Brother? The abbot has seen it, but he sees nothing.

'Who is she, Antonio?'

The young man smiled.

'She is from the village, a girl of sixteen years. Her mother was Sicilian. A girl of Sicilia can pass for a Jewess. I pay her in bread and coin to sit for me. She is an angel.'

'Be careful, Antonio. She is not an angel. And to her, a young man with talent and learning, even in the habit of a monk, might seem little short of a god. How do you get her past Tomassi?'

Brother Tomassi was San Giovanni's prior—wearer of a much publicised secret hairshirt and maker of strict adjuncts to Benedict's Rule.

'I don't. I visit her in her home.'

'Her father—?'

'She has no father.'

'You know what the Eastern Church says of naturalistic painting.'

'Are they right?'

'Between you and me, I think they remain right in many matters where we have gone wrong.'

'I have studied the Byzantine works. Forgive me, Brother, but they are stiff with conventions. Without fire of holy love.'

'Holy love?' Brother Lucio laughed. A laugh the younger monk did not understand, that came from where he had not been.

'The faces are all alike,' Antonio protested. 'The face of Veronica or Magdalene does as well for Maria. There has been more than one woman in the world! I know the ikons are meant to be transcendent but—'

'They are instrumental. The great painters efface themselves entirely. They leave no personal mark. So the will of God be undistorted.'

'You admire this?'

'Yes, I admire it. More and more. They are right, Antonio.' Lucio turned again to the illumination set before him. 'Yet you may also be right, in your way. But Her expression?'

'Scripture tells us she was troubled.'

'But this is more than troubled.'

'Maria is a village girl whose simple heart desires nothing but peace. What will she think when an Angel of God comes from heaven to set her apart, not only from the girls of the village, which has been her world, but from all Mankind forever—when she is called to be Queen of the Universe? She is frightened, Brother. Before and above all else she is frightened! You remember in your youth, the first time you were asked to sculpt a saint for a chapel? You felt honoured, but weren't there hours before the day came to present your sculpture that you wished your commissioners had left you to your cell and to prayer—I knew this fear with my first Book of Hours. That day is already forgotten. Remember Brother, you were asked to dress a stone, not bear God from your body and intercede between Man and the Almighty forever; to stand on Satan's head at the end of Time! Think of it, Lucio, she is to bear God!' Antonio put his hands together and shook them with excitement, 'carry Him in her own body, suckle Him at her breast. Recall, God has never been seen,—'

'But in Josh—'

'It is said Man must never dare depict *Elohim*. What awful form will He take? The God Maria knows is He of Exodus who drinks sacrificial blood and rumbles at the top of a mountain threatening to destroy all the nations of the world at the slightest provocation. The terror of it, Brother! And more . . . she is a virgin bride. What will she tell Giuseppe? What will she tell her father? Who on earth will believe her? No Brother, she is all Grace, but she is human and repugnance will come fast on the heels of fear.'

'And was your subject also fearful when first called to imitate the Madonna?'

Antonio blushed.

Brother Lucio sighed.

'It is extraordinary,' he admitted, running his thumb along the margin. 'I have seen nothing like it, even in Firenze and Toledo. 'But let us put it away, for it overwhelms me.'

In addition to his canonical prayers Brother Lucio prayed for guidance, for Antonio and for himself. He stayed longer than anyone at prayer, not for greater devotion, but because prayer was difficult for him.

'You looked like a great religious,' said Father Benizi when they stood in the garden that afternoon, 'kneeling all alone with the light falling in upon you. The oblates were impressed. Brother Lucio the Pilgrim has become a celebrity in the monastery.'

Both men smiled. This of being a great religious was said without sarcasm: why Lucio had chosen Benizi for confessor.

Benizi hobbled to one of his vegetable beds and explained to Brother Lucio how the spinach they ate the night before was all but over; how you must only plant in the cold, or warm weather cooling, lest the seeds bolt.

'Bolted spinach is without goodness,' he said, and plucked a leaf to put it in the hand of his silent companion. 'Why do you give me so many interviews, Brother?'

'Do I keep you from your work?'

'No. I only ask.'

Father Benizi was fishing for a further confession. Not out of curiosity. He had noted a new trouble written in Brother Lucio's face in addition to the trouble of yesterday. But the trouble was of a cause Brother Lucio himself could not yet name and there was nothing to confess.

'I admire your work, Father. That is all. It is a comfort to know one man is master of a small part of God's earth.'

'No,' said Benizi. 'There can be no mastery in an art that must answer to the seasons, though the soil here is good and enables me to do much. If a man stood long enough in this bed he might strike root.' He jabbed the earth with his fork. 'I abide with what forces exist.'

'Perhaps that is what I meant, Father.'

They walked below an arbour into open fields and to the head of the mule track.

'Ah,' said Brother Lucio. 'There goes our shepherd.'

'To pasture in the neighbour's field. The Conte de Lasso is good to allow it.'

'I think I will follow him. I feel the need to walk.'

'You might see your young friend on that road.'

'Antonio?'

'The same.'

'It is well. Time in the woods will do him good. He spends too long at his desk. Now *he*, Father, is in danger of becoming a master.'

'God protect him,' Father Benizi smiled.

The shepherd had strung his sheep along the white track that decades of hooves had made across the hilltop to water.

'The shepherd boy will be away past Vespers,' Father Benizi shouted across the widening distance.

'I will do penance in my cell.'

So when neither Brother Lucio nor Antonio was present at Vespers no alarm was raised. When finally the shepherd returned, Lucio alone was with him.

The white-haired and saturnine abbot came to meet Brother Lucio. His only concern was the reputation of his monastery, and there seemed little threat to that in the village.

'You have not seen Antonio?'

'No, Father.'

'Father Benizi said you would bring him with you.'

'Yes, Father. But I did not meet him on the road as we thought. On what errand was he gone?'

'For provisions — illuminating supplies.' The abbot sighed vacantly. 'That boy goes to the village far too often of late for provisions.'

Brother Lucio wondered at the abbot's detachment, at

what paint supplies could possibly be found in the village at this hour.

'I will look for him, Father.'

'No,' the abbot sighed. 'Let him return of his own accord. I will speak with him.'

'If I went——'

'No, Brother Lucio. Let him come when he will come.'

'If he be in trouble, Father?'

The abbot laughed.

'Brother Pilgrim! You go from one side of the known world to the other, yet Antonio spends a few hours long in the village and you worry like an old woman.'

'Forgive me.'

Lucio went to his cell to pray. Every so often he glanced out the window that commanded the north-eastern hills and the little village. His prayers fell into ruts and soon he was only reciting the words while his mind followed another well-worn path . . . the mule track tonight arrived at another village, a village in Andalusia, a white village huddled below the snow-capped Sierra Nevada where a stream ran between the houses and a poor girl who cultivated silkworms for her uncle was standing in the street wearing her finest dress, which was not very fine, for the morning Mass. She had an Arabic patronymic, black hair that was brushed by the mountain wind, and green eyes that flashed and stared right through him. They were the eyes he would carve into the weeping Virgin in the *Basilica de la Macarena* in Sevilla. But on this cherished day he stood beside her in her hillside village with no need to remember her face by any art. They stood on a white path that ran through an orchard. That path went all the way to Cadíz and Tangier, yet he was happy picking roadside oranges with she who was beside him and he did not desire to take one step further . . .

He heard scuttling feet and agitated voices and knew Antonio had returned. The young monk looked as wild as a hill man: grass seed in his habit, and face and hands black with charcoal. A scroll of papyrus was under his arm. He took Lucio's arm and led him to the chapel where he lit a candle and spread the papyrus on the ambo.

There were two charcoal sketches, smudged by the artist's impassioned hand. A woman and child were depicted in the first; and in the second, Maria below the Cross. The furnishings for each scene were included in the most rudimentary form. Only the Virgin's face and pose were carefully wrought, and then so much reworked as to be confusing. Lucio wondered how long each sketch required and measured it against Antonio's absence. But perhaps he had poured all his passion into the sketches.

'No,' said Brother Antonio, rolling the papyrus. 'I'm a fool to show you now. But in the coming days, Brother Pilgrim, you will see them as I do.'

Brother Tomassi had been kneeling in the dark at the back of the chapel, extending Compline as his piety demanded.

'I'm surprised even you bring pictures of your tart into the chapel, Brother Illuminator.'

'Is that how you call the *Stabat Mater Dolorosa*, old Pharisee?'

'No. That is how I call the daughter of a drunken swineherd. One cannot stand in the village market more than a few minutes without hearing about your affair in some woman's gossip.'

'It is comforting to know that while God has ceased visiting the sins of the fathers on the children, you have maintained the tradition on His behalf.'

'It will not be I who judges you,' the elder monk grunted.

'Fool,' cried Antonio rising. 'Go back to your pious prayers. Perhaps God will stay and hear you, but I have not His Grace. You must mention those parts of His creation that are not to your taste. Perhaps you will achieve an amendment.'

Brother Lucio led Antonio out of the chapel by the arm to the east wing of the dormitory that contained both their cells.

'You told me she had no father.'

'She has none to speak of. None she acknowledges. Every Sabbath I give the brute a few coins of the baron's commission, to keep him in the tavern and away from his wife and child. If I don't, he beats and steals from them.'

Antonio was in a passion and Brother Lucio knew there was nothing to do but let it burn out.

They passed the refectory. On the table was a half-bottle of wine the cellarer had forgotten to put away. Lucio mentioned it.

'It will help you sleep.'

Antonio laughed.

'Thank you, but I do not need rest.'

Brother Lucio was early to the morning meal the next day. The bottle of wine was still on the table, a cup shy of what it had been at meal's end last night.

When the junior oblates finished their preparations he entertained them with tales. He told them of great cities, of the bands of Almohads who had robbed him on the roads in Andalusia; of Segovia and the fighting bulls that were nothing like the soft white Italian cattle but black and fierce as wolves.

Brother Maieul, the cook, brought Lucio Arabica coffee ground of beans he had brought back with him.

'Ah, God's blessing on you, Brother.'

'You are not filling their heads with nonsense, Brother Pilgrim?'

'Of course. But what else will boys hear?'

'Why do you walk so far, Brother Lucio?' one of the oblates asked. 'All around the earth, they say!'

'To atone for past sins,' said Brother Maieul whose kind eyes did not see a yard beyond his own affairs at the monastery.

'What sins?' asked the youngest, curly-headed oblate.

'Once I was a bandit.'

'No!' the boys cried.

'It is so,' smiled Brother Maieul. 'I have it on good authority.'

'I stole a precious jewel from the Princess of Spain.'

'How did you get away with it?'

Brother Lucio pinched the sleeve of his habit.

'Even the court of Spain will not pursue a criminal to the house of God.' He stopped smiling. 'Christ died for wrongdoers. The more we sin, as I have seen, the more protection we receive. It is the innocent who suffer.'

'Will you travel again, Brother?' — 'Can I come with you?' — 'How far will you walk upon the round earth?' — 'Is the earth truly round, as the old monks say?' — 'Can one walk till he is upside down?' — 'No, I would get a headache. Even when yesterday you held my feet to steal those sparrowhawk's eggs it was so.'

Brother Maieul hurried the boys to their own table as the monks had begun to arrive and be seated.

Lucio finished his meal and Antonio had not come down.

The abbot sent for Brother Antonio to inform him

that Baron Rinaldi of Cosenza was coming to the monastery and wished to see the progress of his *Luke*. Antonio took Brother Lucio's hand and they took the stairs to the scriptorium.

'I want you to see it before Rinaldi,' he said as he laid his hands on the vellum. 'My Nativity.'

'You worked through the night?'

'How could I not? With the guidance of God's light.' He pointed to the row of half-burnt liturgical candles on the desk head. Brother Lucio thought it must have been like the chamber of the Holy of Holies in so much candlelight.

'And yet,' said Brother Antonio, 'you look more tired than I feel.'

'My mind would not stop walking. Last night it walked after you, amongst other ways. But let us see the fruit of your labours.'

Only a very little light trickled in through the window. Antonio re-lit his candles and moved aside. Lucio did not examine the picture for detail as he had the last time. Instead he contemplated the single two-part figure right of centre: the Virgin Mother's pale soot-blackened face, the sweat-drenched hair that touched the forehead of her child, all the pain and fear of the Annunciation transformed into joy.

Antonio stopped smiling when he saw his friend's hands tremble and saw that the man of thirty-eight years was crying. Brother Lucio pushed the page further forward on the desk, to where he could view the picture without staining it with tears. Antonio knelt down.

'You have a great devotion to the Virgin, Brother?'

'Yes,' breathed Lucio. 'That is it. I sometimes think it would mean more that She forgive me than Christ.'

Antonio's eyes widened. He thought Lucio was near to sobbing like a child.

'Oh, Brother,' whispered Lucio, 'If ever I meet her I will turn my face away.' He put his hand over his eyes. 'It would be enough for me to be given Hell and allowed one blessed moment in every thousand years to look up into heaven and see Her happy and beautiful.'

Brother Lucio spoke no more and Antonio felt as he thought the Fathers must feel in the confessional.

The bell for prayer bade them rise. Brother Lucio said he could not. Antonio asked if he wished to move to the window to pray, as he himself sometimes did, to be reminded of glory by the dawn. Brother Lucio said that the village would distract him. He would kneel at the desk.

In three days Baron Rinaldi, famed collector of beauties, arrived at the monastery. The baron was shown various frescoes and statues of saints. He looked upon them with the same indifference he showed all things that did not and could not belong to him. The party made its way to the light-filled scriptorium where the baron was to see his Gospel.

Meanwhile Brother Lucio was at the edge of the woods watching the same light held in a spider's web. Even there the furore reached him. He hurried to the monastery in time to see the baron mount his horse and wave his finger at both the abbot and Antonio.

'Had I known I was getting work from a street artist,' he shouted, 'I would not have bought it so dear.'

'The pages you disapproved will be redone,' said the abbot.

Antonio wanted to argue, but the abbot raised his hand.

Brother Lucio took Antonio's arm and led him along a path to the cliff and the pacifying presence of the ocean.

'It cannot be unexpected,' Brother Lucio consoled.

'What? The existence of such a dunce? You try to prepare yourself for it, but the reality is still shocking.'

'Give him what he wants, Brother. Then—'

'What he wants is ordinary. It is not God's work. How can I turn my hand to it?'

'I was about to say you can keep the pages yourself. So they will not find a book and a public, they will still be what they are.'

'Yes, yes,' said Antonio, quickening his step in measure with his mind. 'But I wanted to immortalise . . .'

'For Heaven's sake why?'

'You don't know?'

'I did once. But nothing Man makes is immortal. And it is a poor immortality that the subject cannot take part in. I prefer our Saviour's. What of her you invest in a book, time will destroy. It is very patient. Even Helen has collected a little dust Homer will never brush away.' Brother Lucio sighed and looked out to sea. 'Let us do our work in the time God has given us, then let time erode it. If we inhabit the world we make too completely we may share its death.'

The monks had drawn close enough to the cliff to see the foaming crests of waves that crashed against its foot.

'I will have my revenge, Brother. I will paint his gospel full of the milkmaid Turello, the wench who sells herself for sweet wine and cakes so her arse may be yet fatter to please the travelling merchants. She has a touch of the classical vulgarity. She will suit the baron's taste.'

Brother Lucio shook his head.

'That is an evil thought, Antonio. The milkmaid is a

child of God. And you must not parody the Virgin. It would be a grievous sin.'

Antonio sighed.

'You are right as ever, Brother Pilgrim. Not the Virgin then. She can come from the Eastern tradition—the ossified memory of some other man's work. But the baron shall have the milkmaid as an angel. No, in a flock of angels!'

'No good comes of vengeance, Antonio. I beg you not to do it.'

But a wave crashed against the cliff and drowned his voice and Antonio turned and sped from him, back toward the monastery.

Brother Lucio had a broken sleep again that night. After midnight prayers he stood at the window like a blind sentry, faced the cliff and the ocean and listened to the waves and ocean wind. If his weak eyes descried some movement it was the Count de Lasso's goats that walked so hard against the edge. When he lay down in the small hours he dreamed of Antonio's *Stabat Mater*, the picture he had not seen but in a rough charcoal sketch. He envisioned it, as he knew it must be, though paint never discover it: the woman still beautiful by virtue of Grace, pleading with Her son, Whom She knew was master of all the universe, to bring Himself down off the Cross, to end His suffering and Hers. The expression of the ultimate hour was upon Her, so Her face must show betrayal: the betrayal He had prepared Her for in Galilee when He had pretended not to recognise her; when this hour He had called her woman and told her to call The Apostle son. But, instead, in the final hour all her face showed was unbroken love. And so the Mother Stood.

Brother Lucio rose before the light to tell Antonio of his dream but the young monk was not in his cell. The cloister was strangely empty. Lucio came upon two monks talking ecstatically. They stammered something about fishermen and a girl and Brother Antonio.

Brother Lucio ran to where a group of monks were looking over the precipice, one on his hands and knees for vertigo. Lucio saw a pair of fishermen who belonged to a felucca in the cove. The fishermen were carrying a white bundle up the cliff-face goat track. The fisherman laid the body on the grass. Antonio knelt over the dead girl and washed her face with tears and kisses as though these might restore blood to her pale face. Through the white nightdress Lucio saw where the girl's ribs had smashed against the rocks before she entered the sea. He sent the goatherd to the village to fetch the girl's mother.

When she arrived the mother fell down beside the daughter who was all she had in the world. The woman wept bitterly and wailed the story of last night to Antonio: how Roso Grella had come home drunk to take what money she and her daughter had made sewing and to take what the monk who sketched his daughter had left. When he found there was little of the first and none of the latter he hit the girl across the face and said that if the monks of San Giovanni were to have use of her like a common whore the least she could do was charge a proper rate so her father could drown his shame in drink. The girl fought him off and protested that Antonio had never touched her; that he painted her as the Virgin and called her an angel; that he said the day was coming when he would leave the monastery and they would live in the world as man and wife. At this her father took her by the hair and dragged her to the Ugolino stables where her saint, as the swineherd had seen on his way back from the tavern, was sketching the town harlot by lamplight with her skirts up around her hips. He had dragged her to that window and the girl had not come home . . .

The monks carried mother and child to the monastery. They wrapped the dead girl in linen and laid her on the dining table.

The Vigil for the Dead, not the Prayers of Penance, was to be attended that night.

'A suicide,' said the village mayor when he arrived. 'That must be noted for the record.'

'She fell,' said Brother Lucio.

'You must see—'

'She fell. I often saw her walking along the edge of the cliffs. The wind is strong here at night. Come back this evening and walk against the edge and see for yourself.'

At Lucio's request Father Benizi would preside at the Vigil.

In the night Brother Lucio and Brother Antonio sat together in the transept watching the altar and the Paschal candle mark an hour of the same flame that burned in every candle ever: 'It seems the same, don't you think, Brother? All things are changeful but that light.'

Brother Lucio nodded. 'There is only one light in the world.'

'You should have seen my *Stabat Mater*,' said Antonio, turning his eyes to the floor.

'Is it made?'

'No. Only in my heart. I was going to paint it . . . but it is a poor immortality.'

Brother Lucio nodded again.

'There is only one of Adam's Nation made Queen of Angels, as there was only one Christ. Perhaps it is best that the face in the ikons is no one; then it can be Maria, because it is not another. Truly, if they are not God and

Queen Angel, then the story is even stranger, for we know what it is to be Men. We do not stand. We are *non stabat*. We fall and fall.'

Both men's eyes travelled between the ground and the candle. They were sharing a purgatory they would never be rid of in this life, nor desire to be.

'You will go away?' Antonio guessed.

'In a day or two.'

'To Iberia again?'

Brother Lucio looked up and into the eyes of the younger and imagined Antonio knew. He could not have. Yet the idea was a comfort.

'There is a leper colony in the East I have promised a Father to give a year to. Finally, I will go wherever the road will take me. I cannot sit still very long, Brother. The mark of Cain is upon me. God will go with me, as he did with my lonely father.'

Antonio asked if they might take the road east together, for companionship, though somehow he knew the answer would be no. He knew Brother Lucio would ever travel alone.

The City Lost to Heaven

*And, behold, the Lord passed by, and a great and strong wind
rent the mountains, and brake in pieces the rocks before the
Lord; but the Lord was not in the wind: and after the wind
an earthquake; but the Lord was not in the earthquake: And
after the earthquake a fire; but the Lord was not in the fire:
and after the fire, a still small voice.*

—Kings 1 19.11/12

I WRITE TONIGHT IN a hotel room supplied by two
congenial governments, having declined the evening's
obligatory prostitute. My window looks across an ocean
of stray light. Chaotic currents up-drift into the satellite
maps I know of Beijing, where light hovers above the
landmass in meaningful, portentous colours. There are
no stars. I squint at a street lamp to prove that curious
accident, that every light, but the thinner the light and
the thicker the surrounding darkness the more, turns into
the Cross . . .

Officially, I am part of a disembodied team of 'foreign
experts' here to advise the Central Committee on preparations for the Olympics: my fields are noise and light pollution. An article on wader migration and artificial light
cast from shoreline developments brought me to wider
attention. My foci were Moreton Bay and a degraded
breeding ground called *Beidaihe*, two hundred and eighty
kilometres east of Beijing on the East-Asian Australasian

Flyway. Truth is, noise and light pollution are such new and unconsidered fields that any papers are notable.

My true reason for returning to China was to find a girl I left here in her first year of study at Beijing Foreign Language University, with whom I lost contact, and who was responsible for the most extraordinary days I shall ever live. Hao Xue's name meant *plenty of snow*. It was given her by the weather on the day of her birth. Now, thirty-years old and embarking upon my third Chinese winter, I thought Hao Xue might be the translator of Western Literature she had hoped to become, else a diplomat or teacher at a foreign university, and I worried that she might be far from Beijing, the city she introduced me to three years ago.

I dropped my bags at the hotel and took a bus to the East Campus of my old university. I walked off the ragged commercial street of mobile phone dealerships and hairdressers, past a pair of city guards into an aberrantly green setting of faculty buildings amidst groves of Chinese pines and sycamores.

At the administration office I called a reluctant middle-aged woman to the desk. The university's records said that two girls named Hao Xue graduated last year. That, it seemed, was as much as she could say. I wondered if the woman was only being curt with an over-inquisitive foreigner. She told me the university did not keep track of students after graduation. Was there any other way of searching? I told her that Hao Xue was from the hutongs; that she had been on scholarship; that she possessed an extraordinary gift for languages. Privately I remembered her sitting on my bed reading *War & Peace* in Russian and answering my childish questions on Mandarin grammar in perfect English.

Suddenly the woman at the desk seemed offended. She told me China might have a million girls called Hao Xue, a quarter of them probably lived in Beijing.

With the administrator's impossible numbers in mind I asked after Hao Xue at our favourite alleyway restaurant behind the university. I retraced our old path, muddy and broken-paved, where leather-skinned migratory peasants sold produce out of wooden carts under floodlights on even the coldest nights. I sat in the filthy restaurant over a plate of dumplings till dusk settled on the street and the cold dust rose around the peasants in a luminous shroud. Chinese pop music blared from a bar across the road and I remembered Hao Xue singing like a child at the table where I sat now: a song from her mother's country.

I did not take the bus to Xicheng and walk along Houhai Lake to where it all happened; though I felt sure I could have found the place, even after three years. Beijing deceives you into believing it may be familiar. The eye and ear are trapped by concrete monoliths, bleating advertisements, incessant traffic and the light that strays upward from half-cut-off and bare fixtures rendering the heavens all but invisible. The imagination is allowed no latitude and is supplanted by the logical and illusory concentric circles that exist in maps, and the city conceals its gigantic depths in a kind of shadow.

I walked to another part of the central city, the market streets behind Tiananmen Square, and remembered her skipping like a child across the place where Mao Zedong announced the birth of a new China, escaping from there into the labyrinth that is old Beijing, the hutongs that were once her home . . .

∼

Hao Xue passed the unofficial beauty requirement at the university despite her dark south-western skin, which is not admired. Her complexion came from her mother who was of the Naxi people of Yunnan. Her mother and father came to Beijing as migrant workers. They slept in human piles against the cold in the subway and train stations. The man carried coal in the hutongs and the hutong people took pity on his pregnant wife; so Hao Xue had many old 'aunts' who became nannies when a munitions factory drew her parents to work and an accident there made her an orphan.

Before she went to university she was the product of a strange, communal, and now unobtainable education that nurtured her gifts. She could draw as many Chinese characters at twelve as the seventy year old compound calligrapher. I believe it was exposure to a variety of languages—her mother's Naxi, her father's Mandarin and the Mongolian of the compound's migrant workers—that meant she began to grasp the grammar of any language after perusing a single page of writing and could speak and even sing in native accents after they were spoken to her. I had witnessed her recite Rumi to the amazement of Iranian students.

How excessive these feats must seem. Fictions. Yet anyone who has experience of poor and rural China knows the country has an abundance of gifted people pushing water-carts, stacking bricks, selling postcards . . . Perhaps it will make Hao Xue more plausible if I say, like all Chinese students, it was a rare day she did not study ten solid hours in overcrowded libraries and classrooms under the draconian but efficacious discipline of Chinese teachers.

She was assigned to me as a 'language partner' by one Miss Zhang, a Chinese language teacher who had some familial connection with the hutongs and became unofficial caretaker of Hao Xue at the university.

After our nightly study sessions, Hao Xue sat in my room and told me stories from her mother's Dongba religious tradition: a pair of lovers leapt off Jade Dragon Snow Mountain and did not die; not so much as a handful of pine needles could be removed from the forest without the approval of priests; one, or maybe five thousand years ago, people saw a tiger leap across a gorge two kilometres above the Yangtze.

I had seen Tiger-leaping Gorge. No animal could cross it unless it flew. Perhaps the witnesses had seen a large hawk? Or perhaps the tiger had merely jumped from shelf to shelf down the rock face? I offered Hao Xue these possibilities. She disapproved of my doubt and gave me a furrow-browed look, as momentarily sincere as a child.

I did not want to appear dull and over-rational. I told her stories from my own Catholic tradition: of the Incorruptibles and the scars that would not heal on the face of the Black Madonna of Częstochowa. I had an RSV Bible mailed for her. She read the New Testament in a night. I asked her whether she believed what it said.

'Don't you?'

'It's a great work of literature,' I answered. 'The greatest.'

'You told me you were Catholic.'

'I admire the tradition, as I admire all the great traditions of the earth. I admire the intellectual rigor of the Church, and its morality.

So I avoided the question of faith. I explained the dignity I saw in Catholicism and Eastern Orthodoxy as compared with the vociferous new protestant churches, whose ranting could not help but distort and make a lie of anything they espoused.

'But the stories are true,' said Hao Xue. She had seen through my attempt at distraction and cared nothing for schisms and politics.

'How do you know?'

She looked out the window. I too turned to the pines that bent in the wind that came unbroken out of Mongolia. The wind that blew the Gobi desert into the city. 'The sound of the words. The voice. It's beautiful. Can't you hear it? Whatever is most beautiful is true.'

I knew if anyone could hear a resonance in printed words so distantly translated it would be her. It occurred to me that the Gospels she read bore no taint of xenophobic English-speaking middle-classes nor insincere co-option into political rhetoric nor maniacal television preachers nor tired priests hurrying through the liturgy before dinner. For Hao Xue the words of the New Testament were as shocking as they were to the book's authors.

I told Hao Xue of the original Greek codex, how the sayings attributed to Christ are said to reveal syntactical characteristics of the Aramaic spoken in Palestine two millennia ago.

She smiled. And the bending pines meant we should stay inside and talk further in the warmth granted by exposed hot water pipes and jasmine tea.

Hao Xue took every opportunity to return to Beijing's old districts. She never tired of exploring them. She delighted in teasing me, escaping suddenly into alleys and deliberately wandering off if I was distracted by a vendor or *erhu* player. Without her I was soon lost. She would follow me at a distance, obscured in a crowd, to laugh at my helplessness. She would take a path of her own intuition through bustling Donghua market, through courtyards and narrow lanes to appear as if by magic on my path, sitting next to a pair of old men playing checkers, or turn from a group of flag waving tourists at the windswept edge of Tiananmen Square.

One evening shortly before I was to leave found us playing this game beneath a red sunset choked by pollution. A current of bicycles, taxis and dilapidated buses flowed in the drizzling light. The city stank with summer heat and night came as a relief. Hao Xue led me up a flight of stone stairs, through a series of short turns, across a stone bridge, and we stumbled into a brothel street.

The girls did not lean rakishly against walls in silky red *qipaos* as they do in films — their profession is illegal in China and is respectfully modest. They stayed hidden indoors (regrettably I knew) in cheap blue jeans and t-shirts. Red lanterns hanging from winged eaves and the grotesque madams beneath them said the place was what it was.

The dusty orange sky silhouetted a row of silver poplars lining the canal. The madams stepped discretely into the lane if a well dressed man and certainly if a young unaccompanied foreigner walked by.

With a single sharp word, Hao Xue dissuaded the old woman who had latched onto me.

A tall, middle-aged European man walked out of a grubby boudoir. The madam of the house followed, perhaps to invite him back tomorrow or tell him of a younger girl who might please him more, perhaps a girl brought on false pretences from the south-west of Hao Xue's blood, who had expected to be working in a theme park or fashion boutique.

A drunken pair of suits stumbled laughing onto the esplanade and were seized and escorted into the first door. Hao Xue furrowed her brow.

I sighed and turned away.

I followed the lambency along the water to a curled-up beggar whose stillness had made him invisible. I had seen the man before—he was hard to forget—in various haunts of the old city, head down in shame and hands cupped above his head as though in prayer to the middle classes that stepped over him. Often he sat on bridges with the prostitutes who did not belong to a house. I guessed he had come to the only place he knew that was frequented by foreigners and where there were no police? But I realised he was not begging. He was not facing the houses of commerce but instead down the waterway. I wondered if he knew someone across the road, a sister. He was shirtless in the heat and I saw the infected abscesses that covered his body.

I turned and saw all Hao Xue's anger had turned to compassion for the man whose disease made it impossible even to tell his age. A tear described her cheek. Like the General in the Tolstoy novel she read, she cried very readily. I followed her steps toward the man. An interval of quiet arrived. The man's troubled breath told that every moment of existence was a torment. Then the sound of his breathing was drowned by a pack of blonde revellers. When they saw the man at their feet they leapt away and cursed.

I took a hundred yuan note from my wallet, but before I could hand it to Hao Xue she had the man in her arms. Just then a madam grabbed me by the sleeve. She showed me a picture of a pretty girl on her mobile phone and told me that the girl was inside the door she pointed at. The woman tried to persuade me, and I listened for politeness. So it was only out the corner of my eye that I saw another girl go to her knees and touch the face of a stricken creature, deemed a bad advertisement even by the women of the street who had chased him into the shadows; and it was only below the hawking of the madam that I heard the girl speak the two thousand-year old name of a Palestinian carpenter's son in Chinese syllables. I turned to see Hao Xue kiss the sick man's cheek.

Poor girl, I thought, and I wondered what I had done by giving her a Bible.

Now she made the sign of the cross as I had taught her, but not over herself—instead over the man, blessing him as though she were a priest. Perhaps, unintentionally, I had become a carrier of false hope. And even then, of a vulgarised false hope: I wondered what religious authority would approve blessings given by a little Chinese girl who had never set foot in a church.

I sighed. I do not know if it was sentimentality or sympathy, but I did not dissuade Hao Xue. I took her arm and we walked back toward the pretty lights of the new town and fashionable Wangfujing.

A week later I walked the same street. I was leaving China the next day and was feeling the hollow regret I always feel at leaving a place I have made a temporary home in. Hao Xue and I had said our goodbyes. She had gone south to visit an old uncle to whom she sent some of her scholarship money. As soon as she was gone I wondered why I had never tried to turn our friendship into something more.

My intention on the street tonight was pathetic. Simply to be excited by the proximity of brothels—to receive the offer I would not accept.

An old madam tried to pull me toward her door. But a crowd of street children were gathered around a man kneeling in the shadows beside the river. Somehow I knew it was the sick man of that night with Hao Xue. I thought the children must be teasing him. I went to break the party up. A street girl's wild eyes turned upon me and I was confused. For the children stood around a man I recognised but whose eyes were as clear of pain as his body was of blemish. Why did I look to the wall of madams and wealthy men, for one of those citizens of the world to confirm a miracle?

Instead, the poor street children and I alone were witnesses.

'Is this the man,' I said frantically to the children. 'Before — he was sick.'

The voices whispered.

'Yes, yes . . . *Shi, shi*' — that word means 'to be' and always sounds like a whisper in Chinese, as though existence itself was a secret — 'This is the man. Yes, yes. Even this morning he was sick.'

The healed man's eyes met mine. Was it him? I was sure it was. I was almost sure. I remembered Hao Xue's blessing, her touching the man's sores. I leaned to touch the man's face myself, but an old woman took me by the arm. She was not a madam, she wore no garish makeup. The street children called her *Nainai*, so she was grandmother to them. The old woman pressed my hand and led me through a narrow concrete archway into the old lanes. The old woman and I moved through the light and dark of the hutongs, her broken voice repeating that I must tell no one of the man. And I promised. A promise I have kept until now, when I believe I am freed from it.

My second day in Beijing found me on a street in Haidian. It was late afternoon and the air was bitter cold and my breath turned to smoke. The university was not far from here and I felt nostalgic watching the bicycles, fewer than three years ago, returning to the hovels, sour bed-sits and awful tenements of their owners. I was with three government men: an advisor whose capacity I never discovered, a man from the Beijing Municipal Environmental Protection Bureau, and one from the Lighting and Advertising Department.

The men admitted that they did not believe light and noise were true pollutants. 'They leave no remnant effect,' said the balding man from the EPB. 'And after all, we can always switch off. Then the problems will disappear.'

How seductive this illusion of control. How difficult to prove an addiction that is not physical. How difficult to argue, in scientific terms, that we will never switch off.

At dusk we examined a street of contesting residences and commerce cut by a main thoroughfare. I pointed out an unnecessary cluster of lamps that at a dip and rise in the road exposed motorists to unshielded light. I explained how that and the plethora of billboards could disorient and create traffic accidents.

'Will or could?'

'Could,' I said honestly.

The man from the Lighting and Advertising Department scribbled briefly in his notebook.

I pointed out the needless over-illumination of empty office blocks and a semi-commercial arcade. But the men protested this last was a walkway for business people moving from the crowded subway station to their apartments. The place is full of thieves, they said. Honest people demanded light for security. I explained how cluttered lights create glare; how glare created shadows for criminals. The men stared at me in silence and I realised I was being taken for a fool.

I gave them statistics — equivalents of energy wastage in barrels of oil.

I mentioned the lesser known effects of continued exposure to the eighty decibels of noise my meter read on the street: increased incidence of neural and cardio-vascular disease, and even the strange, as yet inexplicable, insistence of bad memories. Hopelessly, I suggested city planners and a team of acoustic engineers and designers I knew in Berlin. And I wondered in what obscure file in which one of the thousands of government buildings the report I made to the Committee would shortly rest.

When the men were gone I sat in a cafe at Gongzhufen transit centre and watched dilapidated buses peeling from ranks, packed tight with passengers. Being in those cans was not so unpleasant now in winter. The passengers were mostly labourers, some students, and women shopping for the evening meal. The workers stood with their tools: shovels, picks and sledgehammers tied up in Hessian sacks. They wore blue flannel or the cheap business suits they laboured in day after day. The buses threw cold dust over them and each waited for the one that would take him to his nook of the labyrinth. Some of the students standing beside the workers were immaculately dressed, and some of the girls, I knew, were very beautiful, though I could not see their faces from here. At that realisation the city echoed the awful redundancy of the *Dream of the Red Chamber*, with its exhausting retinue of more-or-less like characters; or worse, the *Classic of Mountains and Seas*, where entry after entry, page after page, landscapes, men, gods and animals are catalogued and distinguished by a mere shuffling of physical attributes. It is the book no one man could ever have written, or read, let alone understood. Laying its unmeaning map upon the city I felt a sense of hopelessness.

The weather turned bitter cold. I thought it would

snow tonight, or one night soon. I was finished my coffee and about to walk to the subway when I felt she was close by. As though she had whispered to me, and though I did not catch the words, I recognised the timbre of the voice. A candle of memory had been lit by this unremarkable place where we were once together. I looked around the café. I hurried out the door and spoke her name on the street. There were dark haired girls aplenty passing by, but none turned. I felt a fool. Two old men who sat out front of the cafe to absorb the warmth in the glass were staring at me.

A windblown night was forgotten by a pleasant Beijing morning. Still cold, but the yellow sun shone and even the city's concrete took on a happier tint. I continued my search for Hao Xue.

I met Jan Gorskopf, once a classmate, now a German diplomat still living in the city. He had heard nothing of Hao Xue since the old days. I tried to find Miss Zhang, her former custodian and teacher, but apparently she had left the University for a post in Chengdu. I was given a phone number that rang dead each of the dozen times I called it.

I took a bus to Tiananmen and walked to the east city hutongs where Hao Xue was from. I cannot be alone in remembering a place so fondly you fear to enter it. I feared change: particularly, a stone wall bearing the white-painted character that meant 'demolish', or worse, her hutong might already be gone. But the place I remembered had survived, albeit shabby and lonely with desertion.

I wandered aimlessly beside lamp-lit games of mah-jong and checkers, avoiding those dark threads where the hutongs were abandoned to ghosts. I entered lanes so narrow they barely admitted my frame. Smells of fish, raw sewage, and wood and coal smoke co-mingled. Women roasted sweet potatoes in fire-drums and children and old men came to warm their hands. I mentioned Hao Xue's name at the fire-drums but the people shook their heads. I spoke to the black-faced coal-carrying boys who had probably not seen more than a few days school in their lives and who laughed at the novelty of a foreigner. I became disoriented. Instead of asking after Hao Xue I found myself asking an old cobbler the way back to one of the places I knew. A few guttural words of Mandarin and contradictory hand gestures made the way no clearer.

I was at the frayed edge of the hutongs, where concrete and ill-laid bricks replaced cobblestones and the sounds of people were drowned by those of machines. The light of incandescent lamps lay like stagnant water, making banks of shadow. A crowd of people came flushing through from a modern avenue and a bicycle crashed into me and sent me sprawling to the ground. I picked myself up and was face to face with a deeply apologetic middle-aged man who had flung his bicycle aside. He took hold of my elbow. Apparently I had come down on a jagged brick. Blood seeped through my shirt. The man took me to a tap to wash out the grit. I assured him I would be fine. Nonetheless he invited me to his home, to have my wound tended by his daughter. He said his name was Lu Yaodong. His accent was a little less throaty than the blue-collar Beijingese. I guessed he had been educated. He pushed reluctant wisps of greying hair from a sallow face that was stretched over sharp cheek bones. He straightened his coat and collected his bicycle and pointed to the bag support where I should sit. I asked where we were going.

'*Jinyu* hutong,' he said. 'Golden Fish.'

The classic circular entrance ways appeared. Lanterns hung from the branches of sycamore and gingko trees. We entered a lane, then a narrow brick archway crested with a blue-stained fanlight. Finches fluttered against the withes of a hanging cage before a wooden door. This was one of the classic *siheyuans:* courtyard houses. Lu Yaodong's ancestors had been courtiers. An uncommonly tall, red-nosed Chinaman opened the door and nodded briefly to me. He and Lu Yaodong exchanged a few short words about a bill.

Behind the door was a steam-filled room and a girl whom I supposed was Lu Yaodong's daughter. The girl smiled bashfully at me from across a low table where she knelt laying out the evening meal: dumplings and a fragrant soup. When she stood up from the table I saw that she was lame; her left shin was as curved as a rugby ball. She took a wooden crutch from where it rested on a lattice sill and led me to a basin. She washed my arm and dabbed it with iodine and laughed when I flinched.

Lu Yaodong invited me to eat with them. His daughter, he said, was a fine cook. 'Xiao Lu', Lu Yaodong called her plainly, 'Little Lu', for in China at least a million girls are called 'Little Lu' one hundred times a day. He told me they lived alone. His wife had been dead six years. Xiao Lu was excited at the event of a guest, especially one from a foreign country. Even so she was quiet. After I explained my work for the Olympic committee she became shy, mistaking me for an important man.

'Poor girl,' her father said in front of her. 'I have a chiropractor from the hospital come once a week. Mr. Ling. That was him you saw leaving when we came in. We work at the same hospital and he has taken Xiao Lu as a subject for his research, so it costs me relatively little.

And see, I have moved the kitchen here next to the guest hall for her!'

I saw a pallet of pills on a window sill that must have been hers. I was always shocked by advertisements on Chinese television for pharmaceuticals whose wondrous claims included stimulating adult bone growth, enlarging breasts and increasing one's intelligence by over-activating certain glands. Against the kitchen wall rested a metal brace, also a treatment prescribed by Mr. Ling.

Barely raising her eyes to me the girl introduced the soup of mutton, mint and shellfish—a recipe from Shandong.

Xiao Lu was of marrying age and her deformity troubled her father. 'Only a wealthy man can afford a lame wife,' he said. 'But how she can cook! I'm trying to find her a little restaurateur. She would be very useful to such a man.'

Unlike many of the compound, Lu Yaodong was in no hurry to move to a modern tenement building. He said the hutongs were where his heart was. He told me his story.

As I supposed, he was one of China's lost generation. He had been taken from university and his study of architecture and sent to work in Guizhou province. In 1977, no longer a young man, he married and returned to Beijing and a job at the hospital. Lu Yaodong regretted he was forty-five years older than his daughter. He earned only a low-level hospital administrator's wage. His lungs were not good. What would become of Xiao Lu if he became sick?

When the food had satisfied him Lu Yaodong disappeared behind a wall, leaving me to a few bashful moments with Xiao Lu. He returned with bottles of Qingdao beer and a packet of French cigarettes. We talked of the hutongs.

'More destroyed each day,' he lamented.

Of course, I had waited for the moment to bring up what was always on my mind.

'I knew a girl who was born here,' I said. 'Here in the east city hutongs.'

'Oh, yes?' smiled Lu Yaodong.

'Her name was Hao Xue.'

And even the girl who knelt husking corn stopped and looked up at me. Lu Yaodong's look of geniality was replaced by one of suspicion.

'You knew her?'

'I was her friend at university.'

'Yes. Hao Xue went to university.'

'Has she graduated?'

'She never got that chance. You see . . .' but the man paused. Even a foreigner these days may not be safe to talk to, particularly one who spoke Mandarin and admitted to being on the government payroll.

'Hao Xue was very special,' he said. 'She—'

'Could cure the sick,' I said rashly. I expected a denial. Laughter.

Instead the eyes of father and daughter met in silence. Lu Yaodong stubbed out his cigarette and asked me directly: was I *Wo'di* or *Tianzhujioade*? I did not recognise the first word—tonight I know it means 'secret police'. The second meant Catholic.

'I am Hao Xue's friend,' I told him. 'Nothing more or less. I loved her.' I had never admitted so much even to myself. 'I lost touch with her after I returned to my country.'

Lu Yaodong lit another cigarette and spoke in tones I thought unnecessarily hushed:

'We of the hutong kept the strange stories that sur-
rounded Hao Xue very quiet. She would go from here
with a man who wore a hood against the winter. She
would go on the subway to Qiananmen and Nantang
Cathedral. The hooded one was a religious from Poland.
Hao Xue spoke with him regularly. There was no law
against it. At least none that the government chose to
enforce, which amounts to the same. But then Hao Xue
contracted a disease. She was so often among the poor and
sick. A disease of the skin.'

I sighed at the injustice. I blamed myself and my Bible.
Was she still sick? Lu Yaodong could not say. And the
nature of the disease — did it effect her face? I recalled
with regret the wild eyes and earth-coloured skin she had
in common with the mountain girls I had seen in her
mother's home.

'Her hands,' said Lu Yaodong, holding out his palms,
'and her feet. She would not stop bleeding.'

I do not know how long I sat in silence with my breath
stuck in my chest.

'Hao Xue refused the doctor,' said Lu. 'Rumour of
the strange disease leaked out. I think people were concerned for her. She stayed in the hutongs more than ever.
Finally, she had to be hidden even here. Poor people
began sitting in the lanes as though they belonged, but
whose homes and names were unknown and whose hands
were without marks of work. Questions of Hao Xue were
always in their talk. On the last night I ever saw her,
the hooded man from Nantang was here. I was walking
home and happened to peer through a window into the
home of an old seamstress. There I saw the hooded one
making a compress for Hao Xue's hands. He wept with
great apology in his face, but first he spoke words I could

not hear and he kissed her hands and feet and even her stomach without fear of contagion.

'You saw—the disease?'

'They were deep sores, friend. I saw twice with my own eyes how deep! But, strangely, those nearest her said they never festered or spread and there was no smell of corruption. That last night I stayed long enough to see the dressing of her wounds and a session of prayer begin. I left a couple of old women at the window. The women said the hooded one took Hao Xue back to Nantang before morning. It was not unusual for her to be gone for days, but then a policeman came to the hutongs asking for the names of all those who were friends of the girl Hao Xue, spreading the story that the disease was not a disease and that Hao Xue was insane—that she made the sores herself with acid.'

At this point Xiao Lu hobbled to the table. Her eyes were wet with unfallen tears. 'Hao Xue was not insane, was she? She said she would cure me. The God she prayed to, it is your God, yes?'

I told her every good thing that was said about Hao Xue was true and every evil thing was a lie. Lu Yaodong shooed the girl away into the courtyard.

'Hao Xue knew of my daughter and our troubles. Once like thunder out of sunshine she said, "Before I die Xiao Lu will walk as I do, Lao Lu". Like a fool I told the girl.' He pointed to the wall that concealed his cripple daughter.

Apparently Lu Yaodong was hard of hearing as he did not turn when poor Xiao Lu made her best attempt at stepping quietly to the doorway she was banished from. Her boyish haircut and plain face appeared and I gave her a smile over her father's shoulder.

'Understand, we loved Hao Xue, even those of us who

83

did not believe in her gifts. But the children here were not to mention her name. The policeman gave them sweets and instructions — a telephone number and a meeting place — should they hear their parents mention the crazy woman, Hao Xue, the witch who made magic with her own blood. Finally, a story reached the hutongs that she had been taken from the hooded one at Nantang and her whereabouts were unknown. Then the Catholics got rid of the hooded man, who was said to be in disgrace. No one has seen or heard from Hao Xue since.'

Even those of us who did not believe. Lu Yaodong's phrase resounded in my mind. I thought of the prodigy I had witnessed. Had I been tricked by the light that night? Perhaps the man had not been as sick as he appeared now in my memory. Perhaps he had not been as cured. Perhaps, after all, it had been a different man surrounded by the children. I knew what specious light memory casts on the past, and my memory is especially fallible.

But now there was the story of the wounds. Hao Xue had the most fertile imagination I had ever encountered. There were those who claimed St Pio's wounds were the result of autosuggestion. Tests to recreate such wounds had resulted in nothing more significant than sweat, but perhaps, after all, it was not impossible for an imagination of great power . . .

'You don't believe the stories?' I said to Lu Yaodong.

The man sighed.

'Sometimes the great want of something, the need for it to be, can make it appear as if it is, when we see only our desire. Secretly I have thought this about myself and Hao Xue: if it was only for the sake of my daughter . . .'

'But you saw . . .'

'What did I see? I heard rumours of healings. I saw a hooded man kiss a girl's bleeding hands and make prayers.

But the girl herself was not cured! Quite probably she's—'
He stopped and lowered his eyes. 'In the end these are
all I have. How can I, a poor half-educated man, make
any sense of this world? Only, Hao Xue was not insane.
That is the one thing I know for certain. That one thing
troubles me.'

We had exhausted our knowledge of Hao Xue. Darkness bedded in the abandoned rooms of the house. A
lantern lit the emptiness of the courtyard. I thanked Lu
Yaodong and his daughter for their hospitality. Lu made
me promise to return before I left the city.

The next day I tried to arrange an interview with the
bishop at Nantang. A lay assistant regretted that the bishop
and all the priests were busy and would be indefinitely.
I looked up a Macau-born friend I had made those years
ago reading copy for the *People's Daily*. It was a relief to
speak English. I asked Juan if he had heard the story of
Hao Xue, perhaps he had seen her with me in the old
days? Though I realised now I had jealously guarded her.

'The girl from the hutongs,' I said.

He had heard of her mysteries.

'You didn't run the story at the *Daily*.'

Juan lit a cigarette and smiled wryly at my need to ask.

'Look up "stigmata" in a dictionary here. You'll get
the meanings for 'stigma': 'to be marked with a hot iron'
first; then 'moral disgrace'. The story wouldn't have made
sense. I went over there myself. I remembered the name
in association with you and wondered if it could be the
same girl. But the truth is there wasn't much of a story to
tell. Innuendo, conflicting rumours, the official accusa-
tions of immolation; official statements are harder to track
to one man than rumours. No one was willing to defini-
tively say anything. I don't understand what the Central

Committee has to worry about. She represented your executed criminal god—it's unlikely such an unprosperous god would ever take hold here.'

No less likely than in my country, I thought. 'My country has set up Baal in Christ's place, though the names get confused. A man who ran as a Palestinian mystic with no fixed address or money would not see a day outside barbwire if he landed in Australia.'

Juan tapped cigarette ash into a tray and whistled to a bleary eyed waitress.

'Is this Baal a worthy god?'

'He has provided many good harvests. Our people have no reason to complain.'

I mentioned my idea of going to Nantang to surprise a priest and ask after Hao Xue.

'You can try, but the Church is run by patriots. Authentic Catholics rarely contact it these days. Fake bishops are appointed without the approval of Rome. You must have heard? Same as the Tibetan strategy.'

In this restaurant three years ago we two, Jan Gorskopf and others had discussed the infiltrated monastery at Lhasa and the possibility of a Chinese Dalai Llama. A nun had been sniped crossing into Tibet only weeks ago. What use the talk of educated men?

'It's easier to become a bishop or llama than a street sweeper,' Juan joked.

'But the methods the government use for extracting apostasy are no joke.'

'No.' Juan shook his head and commented that it was uncommonly cold tonight.

'You work at a paper. Tell me.'

Of course I had heard of tortures carried out on Buddhist religious and members of Falun Gong. But the

Western media knows little of China's inner workings and is allowed to tell less. Juan was an insider.

He was reluctant. I pushed him.

'I've seen photographs,' he said. 'Electrocution. Men and women tied up with barbed wire. Noise tortures. Burning of hands and feet. I don't truly know.'

And I had the certain feeling he had spared me.

'You Orientals are brutal.'

Juan did me the courtesy of turning to his food and not replying.

I rode the crowded subway to Qiananmen and was once again in the centre of Beijing. Work was going on through the night on a new monolith, larger than any in the district judging by the depth of the foundations. White floodlights pressed a false day down upon the site. Behind a wire hoarding Mongolian and south-western peoples yelled bluntly at each other in the rudiments of their acquired common language that sounded like barking dogs and could express only the demands of the building. I wondered how many lives had been sacrificed to it already. There was at least one for every high-rise. I noted the insidious beauty of the blind sky, the pollution that reflected electric light and became alluring violet, and thought, unforgivably, that this could not be the least pleasant hour to labour.

I walked Qianmen Road to the cathedral. I checked my watch and the notice board. Mass had finished half an hour ago.

A girl passed on the street whose flashing face recalled Lu Yaodong's daughter, but I turned and saw her scuttle down the pedestrian underpass. I lit a taper and placed it before the *Mater Dolorosa* and hoped the light would perpetuate my prayer.

I approached the altar where a young priest was removing his soutane.

'Am I too late, Father?'

The priest told me I should return tomorrow. He stood on his toes to blow out a row of altar candles.

'Actually, I'm not here for Mass. I want to speak to you about a friend of mine. You may know her. A girl named Hao Xue.'

At the name the young man stopped and stared at me. 'That name means nothing to me except a sick person.'

'I'm only trying to find her. I have no interest—'

'In her miracles? There were no miracles. She made her wounds with acid,' he pointed to his palms. 'The age of immolation is long past. She brought dishonour to our Chinese Church.'

'You saw the wounds?'

'No,' he said. 'I never met Hao Xue. She happened before I came here. But I have it on authority—'

'Where is she now, Father?'

'How should I know? I say Mass tomorrow at nine. Come if you have any interest in the Church besides gossip and magic.'

'Just give me a name. One name. Someone who might help me!'

'I don't know one.' He waved me away, blew out the last candle and left via a side door. There was no point following him; I felt he had told me the truth.

I walked outside and stood at the top of the Cathedral stairs. I wondered if any of the night's electric lamps lit that face my memory struggled to light tonight, though it had only been three years . . . if one of the yellow windows, into whose hideous room I feared to allow my thoughts to enter, was hers. A wall of cold Mongolian wind struck my face. I could not go back to the hotel. I knew I would walk the labyrinthine streets, unable to help searching for her face among the thousands of faces I would pass.

I spoke to the starless sky.

'If You are there, why did You give her signs You knew would get her killed in a deaf and blind room, where no one would ever see and believe? Why do You hide Yourself? Come now and save her! Even if I believed in You, I would have no faith in You because You close off every avenue to Your people. You have killed her for nothing, and You have toyed with me. You let every light outshine You; every voice shout over You. We have all of us suffered for nothing. No one believes in Hao Xue now. Not even me. You have achieved nothing.'

I sank into the streets of the unfathomable city like a lost child. Everything was strange and everyone a stranger. Slate-grey building gave way to slate-grey building, blank determined face to its like, till I saw all the city go by a thousand times and not nearly once, and I felt the full brunt of Beijing's immensity, the hopelessness of searching for anyone or thing within it. So I would go to the one house in the city that had invited me.

The long awaited snow began. The snow seemed to lend its silence to the crowded night.

Amazingly, I found the way without a false step.

Lu Yaodong was not home. Once more the chiropractor was leaving as I arrived. He looked like a lost child.

'It's worked,' he whispered.

'What has worked?'

He looked away and furrowed his brow. He looked back and only then seemed to recognise me.

'What's worked?' I repeated.

'All of it,' he stammered. Then his eyes grew clearer.

'Yes, yes,' he said. 'It has been very successful. I must go to make a report.'

The man strode determinedly into the night. I was left at the entrance.

Xiao Lu stood in the open courtyard weeping, the snow slanting down upon her through the light of an orange lantern.

I laid my hand on her face but could not speak.

Her voice shook like my hand.

'I walked to Nantang this afternoon,' she said. 'It was cold so my leg pained more than usual, but I felt I must go. You see, when I heard you speak of Hao Xue, I knew you believed in her, and then I believed in her again too. So I went to the cathedral to pray. A white-robed girl knelt at the altar. I knelt beside her and put my hands together. I saw her face, but closed my eyes. She whispered that my wrongs were undone, and when I stood up she was gone. I felt so well I did not want to ride the bus home. I walked. I was half way home . . .' She looked down at her leg. Her tears fell in a stream. She held a wooden crucifix to her lips.

I did not know the power of the innocent.

'Pray for it to be undone. They will come for you. You will be hurt.'

She shook her head.

So I must put my faith in the chiropractor's report. I felt shame for the painless way I had made through the world. And again I looked to the sky.

Now You've marked a child even smaller and less protected than Hao Xue. Once more You have merely whispered, as You always do through peasants and shepherds and cloistered religious. Why not me? The newspapers would listen to me. Even governments must respect a white-skinned, English speaking scientist. I could give

Your message, whatever it is, the volume to compete with the din of Your enemies. I would be even louder!

Silence was my answer.

A dirty faced urchin came through the open door to deliver a bucket of coal. The boy gasped. Xiao Lu smiled at him.

'It was Hao Xue,' she said.

The boy ran his hand over Xiao Lu's shin, and she allowed his coal-blackened fingers to touch the wooden figure of He who wrote only a few obscure letters in the sand that were blown away.

And the snow fell quietly on the three of us in the courtyard and on the cobblestones and mudded ways without, hushing even the great city. I knew at some point during the night the most painful cries would be enveloped by a gentle whisper.

In the City of Exiles

*for he hath neither ships fitted with oars, nor crew to carry him
so far across the sea . . .*

— *The Odyssey*

IN THE AFTERNOON he had sat down by a cooking
fire with merchants and the soldiers who guarded their
passage into Sidon and been given a crust of stale bread
for one of his greatest sequences: verses that told of a
homesick soldier who must sail past the fatal sirens.

A stubble-bearded captain had humphed down his
nose.

'Memory plays you false old man. I have sailed the
waters you sing of. The only harlots on the sea were
aboard our ship, bought from the slave market in Tyre.
And their only danger lay in the filthiness of their parts.'

The other men laughed.

The captain tore him the crust.

'Bring us wine or women, else go sing your song to
fools.'

The old man's boy took the lyre and the old man's
arm. The boy led him to the top of the quay where he
sat down as he was wont to, squinting into the distance as
though his sightless eyes could still make out the horizons
of the earth. The boy said a flotilla of battleships was in
the passage.

'What ships?'

'Ten of them. Double-banked, with rams, and square sails midship.'

'The ensign?'

'Some kind of hawk — a disk at its heart,' said the boy.

The old man sighed.

'Phoenician triremes, but they belong to Sennacherib now.'

The boy asked the old man if they would go down to talk to the sailors — follow them to a tavern and listen to their talk for tales of new heroes. And perhaps a captain would give them a berth if there was not already a poet aboard.

But the old man shook his head.

'I have no use for the heroes of their ugly new wars.'

The old man had wandered from city to town in the Greek Isles and Phoenicia, selling a night's song for as much as ten gold coins and as little as applause. He had been in Sidon more than a year. All the world passed through Sidon at one time or another, and he came to realise there was no need to wander further after scraps of tales, nor people who were ignorant of his own. In Sidon a transitory audience of princes, soldiers and sailors heard the fragments of epics he recited by campfires and in public houses.

In his youth he had been a soldier. He had sailed on North African cities with the Phoenicians, resting them from Assyria; in Egypt Sennacherib himself fled from his sword. And he had travelled by caravan deep into the heart of the desert, scaled tremendous yellow walls and delivered a citadel from the grip of a roving Babylonian militia.

Sea-glare took his sight. He possessed an impeccable memory, a strong voice and a pretty turn of phrase, and when his eyes failed battleships that had hired him as a warrior kept him aboard to sing. He sang of all he loved and had lost, cast in the glinting bronze of another age. He sang of all that the young sailors stood to gain and that the older men had begun to disbelieve yet some strange melancholy bade them hear. If allowed, he would begin his song at evening and not finish till the second dawn. In his vast poetic country a war was waged for love of a woman, and a hero was abroad, ever trying to find his way home . . .

A hooded, black-bearded man drew along the esplanade. He was headed for the fires on the beach where fresh catch was roasted and sold for a few coppers or the promise of a day's work. He saw the old man sitting with the boy at the quay. Sidon had no shortage of old men — antique soldiers and merchants who had no better home — and he wondered why he was drawn to this one. But when he drew close the attraction became repulsion, as though he was meeting the insurmountable walls of a city greater than Babylon.

The old man listened to the footsteps of the one who came along the path. Hundreds of men walked the esplanade each day, and he wondered why these steps should command his attention. When the steps were close the old man felt overwhelmed, as though a great wind had risen against his ship and was pushing him back from a strange new land. He greeted the visitor in Greek. He was answered in the tongue of King David.

'I thought, by your step, you were Egyptian,' the old man said. 'The Egyptian moves so slowly he will never arrive at the future.'

'Then you have me wrong indeed,' said the black-bearded man. 'I walked slowly because I was trying to recognise you.'

'Do you know me?'

'It is given me to see many things, but you—no. You I have not seen in the world or in dream. What are you called?'

'My name, in this city at least, is Homer. And you, friend?'

'I am Isaiah.'

The old Greek repeated the breathy Hebrew syllables.

'Every wandering soul must pass through this port,' he said, 'the waning city; the rose that bloomed for a moment and wilts for eternity; the city that no king may hold for longer than a season; the camp of exiles. But each man has his own reason for arriving at the crossroads of the world. What brings you to Sidon?'

Isaiah smiled at the poet's epithets. He sat down and looked to the sea.

'I served a good king, but he is dead. His son keeps Sidonian priestesses in his house to hear their soothsaying. He erects altars to stone idols and reddens them with the blood of our children. And we are soon to be scattered, laid to waste by God, whose hand will take the shape of Assyria or Babylon. That is all one. Yet I am hated fiercely for saying so, by king and people alike. How strange that I should be safe here, at the heart of Baal's cult.'

'Not strange. Here every man is a slave of a king, terrible in reputation but far distant, and by virtue of that fact as free as a bird. That and the mountains protect us: like the little yellow flower at your feet, that is found nowhere but here.'

Isaiah looked at his sandals and then at the old man's sightless eyes and laughed.

Homer smiled. 'Not strange. But you mean the cult of Eshoun?'

'Baal, Eshoun, Astarte. They are all one. They all mean

Lord of the World and, yet, nothing. But to answer you, I am waiting.'

'For what?'

'For the future.'

The old man sighed.

'The future is desolate. The past alone is true.'

'The future exists,' said Isaiah. 'I have seen it. Though, somehow, it is infirm, and must be carefully sought. I must wait for it here, till the time is right.'

'And yet,' said Homer, feeling the ground and picking one of those rare yellow flowers. 'I long ago decided it is the past that exists but is infirm; the past that must be carefully sought. Since I lost my eyes I have believed this. In the evenings I sit beside anyone who can pay; my audience takes me for any other bard, singing to remain alive. But what use have I to live longer? No. Each night I take up the thread of the past in the hope that it will lead me back.'

'To where? Some battlefield of youth? I have heard the bloody Greek epics. Fear not, the past has not exhausted the future of wars. You will not be there to slay and be slain, but what is that? Perhaps you follow the cult of honour and wish you had been slain at your height.'

'Yes.' The old man closed his eyes to make his darkness complete. 'Yes, man, you are right. I would be happy to have never lived beyond one day. It was the night after battle. I was in a strange city, in a room in a house of arched doorways. The walls were inscribed with letters that I could not read but were like the shapes that candle-flame carves out of darkness. In my bed was an Aramean dancing girl who was not sorry her masters were defeated. She had been waiting for me, but now it was late and her almond eyes were closed. Gold bangles rattled on her ankles and wrists while she dreamt, and one long dark thigh like a gazelle's lay without the silk sheets. I almost woke her, but my own mother was a dancer for a tyrant, and I let the girl sleep. I was standing on a stone portico. Nothing was on the street but firelight. Even the watchman was drunk and asleep in his tower, for the city was safe, and I stood looking up at the stars that seemed no more wondrous and infinite than my days on earth . . . That is the place I try to find along the thread of my song. That place that was mine and is now barred to me by the iron doors of time.'

'This is the tale you sing?'

Homer shook his head.

'I will never sing it, because I am jealous. If I sing it I fear I will lose it. Yet I allow myself to shape a world around that room that was so foreign and familiar it felt like a long lost home. The world of my poem upholds that one true and glorious point in time and space that threatens to vanish at my death. You see, I am cursed. First with blindness—that does not even allow me the present to set against my past—and cursed doubly with a vast memory. Other men may replace today's losses with tomorrow's hopes, but I know how the world's glories vanish like smoke into the dark.'

'And yet,' said Isaiah, 'For me the past is a bitter well. My people have rarely known peace. Home has been but a brief sojourn between exiles; and slavery and war have been our companions. Now a terrible past has crept into our cities, with the face of Egyptian gods and Baal, even into Jericho and Jerusalem, and turned Men of the Lord into worshippers of chance and stone. For me the past is a scattered, hopeless country. It is the future that fills my thoughts. God pushes me into its barren regions, after a kingdom that haunts my dreams, so I am never satisfied. And so I have lost everything: my country, my people, my wife and son. The poem I carry is too great for mortals. Those whom the God of Israel asks to bear it may know no happiness.' The Jew prized a stone from the ground and threw it into the sea. 'No happiness at all.' He sighed. 'The universe speaks incessantly to me. I see angels in the shape of winged lions that tread behind every man to the poorest of beggars, even to the latrines and the places men toss coins.' He laughed charily. 'One night in Jerusalem, the city under siege and its army outnumbered, my king asked me where was my God. I closed my eyes in fear, for I did not know, and a voice spoke as though through a crack in my head, saying God would repel the Assyrians. I told the king. The Assyrians were two hundred-thousand strong. I knew I was mad. I sat sleepless on the wall that night knowing I would be executed when the city was stormed in the morning, and I watched an Angel of dark flame slay all but a tent-full of the soldiers camped at our gates.' Isaiah shut his eyes on the daylight that was drawing away and wondered had that really been, or was that a day to come. 'And I see a blood debt. This world is falling apart for the evil of men; innocent blood must be the mortar. The debt is too great for men to pay; yet in my poem there is one who will pay it. How will this one's blood may be so precious as to equal all men's blood ever? What terrible, sad thing he will be, God alone knows. And I prepare the way for this one! I am the shadow cast before him, for now we have passed midday and it is the afternoon of the world. But I will never reach the hopeful shore of his making, not before I have slept with Abraham. I will never know your night after battle, only the battle, and a ship comes soon to take me to its heart, and this time to my death. Already the wind snaps the sails of that ship. Only here, in Sidon, for the last time in my life, is the future held at bay. I may glance without intention at pretty foreign girls—for we are all foreign here; I may sit down to meat with soldiers who on other shores would slay me. Here I may have respite.'

'Yes,' Homer agreed. 'Only here, in the city of travellers, despite our contrary natures, are you and I near home. For when a young sailor cuts the wind by my ear with a brass sword, though he found it buried and forgotten and does not know its name . . . when a woman walks by me with tinkling bangles, though she be the plain wife of a tax collector . . . then I hear my place whispering to me. Then I feel it belongs to the memory of the universe, not merely to my own memory, and may be shaped again with the remnants that are left.

'I may dream of the day when a grand ship with the power to sail against the current of time will arrive here, and we all go down to the harbour and throw flowers into the sea, crying out that beauty has returned. And you may sit and dream that another will yet be chosen to do your work, and you will stand on the distant shore of your poem. So you stay here in Sidon with unbroken hope.'

Isaiah nodded.

'But my fatal ship will come.'

'Yes.'

'And your ship will not.'

'No.'

'We are neither of us fit for this world,' said Isaiah with a melancholy smile.

'But we are fit for Sidon.'

The Jew nodded and stood up: 'And now I go to take my meal at ease among strangers.'

'You say you see the future. Are we to meet again?'

Isaiah shook his head.

'We should not have met this once. But God has been merciful and closed his eyes.'

'You mean the fates have been careless.'

'That is all one. Perhaps, though, we will meet once more. In a country where time's hold is broken. Then we will trade stories again.'

'In that country,' said Homer, 'there will be no need.'

The Jew smiled and pulled his hood over his head and walked off toward the bay and the coming centuries, leaving the old Greek alone with his boy, squinting his sightless eyes at a lost sea.

The Lost Country

I AM WRITING IN a motel room in Alice Springs. The GPS receiver fixed to the dash of my Land Cruiser suggested the place. What strange maps we of the 21st Century make. Like all maps, I suppose, they are graphs of desire as much as assessments of geography. But how our desires have diminished: from Ptolemy's mythological heavens and pilgrims' maps of holy ground, to the lie of discount beds and cheap franchise restaurants. How the new maps, updated constantly, hurry memory away into oblivion.

I came to Alice and the Tanami Desert to investigate something I was unable to forget: the death of Ned Miriwoong, that man who either hung himself on the only pale ghost gum in fifty miles of red desert or was hung there. The case was officially closed. Yet the investigator's reports I read in Darwin seemed deliberately vague. It was never explained why a man who possessed a sawn-off .22 rifle should walk three miles across baking red dirt to kill himself by the most horrible means.

'It's a dark country in there,' said one of the old hardheads at headquarters. 'Best leave it to em.'

But three weeks ago, I drove into that sea of red soil and spinifex that is the Tanami in order to conduct my own investigation.

I camped that first night on the side of the road. The next

day I passed through unmemorable country. I stopped at a settlement called Yuendumu, then drove 310km to the next settlement, 280 to the next. I crossed the West Australian Border, as arbitrary an imaginary line as Man ever drew between red earth and red earth. The road became little more than an aqueduct for sand, always threatening to become lost entirely. I turned off for Gurindji aboriginal community at dusk. Burning spinifex bushes dotted the western horizon. Dark figures hurried behind the plywood and corrugated iron shacks into the shadows made by floodlights.

A wiry silver-bearded elder came and shook my hand with suspicion writ in his smoky yellow eyes. I presented my permit and asked him if he had a humpy for a whitefella. He pointed to a plywood hut and said I could stay with the other whitefella.

'The other whitefella?'

'E out bush now. E good young whitefella. E ere paint em pitures.'

The bronze-skinned painter stepped into the humpy an hour later. He appeared to be in his late thirties. His name was Thompson. I discovered he was responsible for the burning spinifex I saw from the road.

'It contains a resin that makes it especially flammable,' he said. He showed me digital photographs of the fires against a dying blue sky. He would paint these tomorrow.

Miniature canvasses were stacked in a corner of the room. Thompson showed me an envelope-sized painting of an orange-crested spinifex pigeon making tracks on red sand. Another of a black sliver hanging from a white tree.

'Is that what you're here about?'

I nodded.

'Perhaps you can help me? You seem to have the elder's trust.'

'I'm considered harmless. But I only know as much about Ned Miriwoong as I painted. I don't speak the local language.'

I unfolded a map of tribal boundaries based on the old Norman B. Tindale designations of 1974.

'These people are Jaru?'

'That's the broad linguistic group. They're one of about a dozen recognised Jaru clans in the Tanami.'

I offered Thompson a drink from one of three bottles of Scotch whisky I had brought for the trip.

He looked at the bottles disapprovingly and shook his head.

'I thought you were a policeman? You know this is a dry camp.'

'It's for my own use.'

I laid my swag out on the floor.

Before sunrise we took water from a bore the government dropped here forty years ago for cattle. One rusting tap and a concrete lid sat above ground. What a precarious existence, I thought. What if this bore should fail one day? What if the pipe started leaking metal? Thompson read my thoughts.

'You see why the water is sacred.'

After a breakfast of porridge, Thompson put a bridle on an Arab-cross pony that stood in a makeshift yard of plain-wire and metal posts at the back of our hut. He packed his paints, a water pouch and three small canvases into a rucksack and rode into the dawn, headed for what he called 'the creek' to see a hermit he called Old Warragul.

'You have to meet Old Warragul,' Thompson beamed.

'He's like no one on earth. And if anyone can help you, he can.'

That day I interviewed every man, woman and child at Gurindji about the death of Ned Miriwoong. I sat around fires, beneath scrubby trees and inside baking shacks of corrugated iron. No one knew anything. But the children I spoke to would not look me in the eye. I became certain that everyone in the settlement was hiding something, but simple questioning was not going to obtain it. Frustrated, I began to curse.

'Why do you want to live in the Dark Ages!' I shouted. 'If there's a killer in this country then let me catch him for you.'

My response was silence.

I felt a fool. For the surest way to get these people to close their mouths is to shout at them.

I sat late that night over black tea at the campfire with Thompson. He showed me a painting of animal tracks that looked like cuneiform. The tracks moved over furrow lines of sand. Thompson said these lasted only a few hours before the Tanami's winds blew them away.

I told him I would have to conduct my investigations further afield, that the people here were secreting something that perhaps another clan would not.

'They won't speak the name of a dead person. Not for years after. Sometimes never. That explains their reticence.'

I sighed. Anyway, I wanted to see the tree where Miriwoong was hung.

'Old Warragul will take you.' Thompson dragged a coal from the fire with his boot to light a cigarette. 'The tree's not far from his humpy. He used to be a tracker. He's taken me places I never could've got to. Outcrops and dunes; strange formations of ant hills; places of old and secret water.'

'Why does he live apart from the others?'

'Thompson shrugged. He's not the same dialect as these at Gurindji. They say he comes from Purnululu.'

'What does he say?'

'That he comes from everywhere.' Thompson smiled and drained tea through a sheet of mesh. 'Maybe he did something wrong and got banished. But that old humpy of his has been down on the creek for ten years. I call him the keeper of the water—though there is no water—not visible anyway. Perhaps he just likes solitude. After all, that's the reason I'm here.' Thompson drew on his cigarette and smiled. 'You know, he's got a cassette player and one tape: Palestrina's *Lamentations of Jeremiah*. I thought he'd pinched them from a station or mission. Something he might be able to trade. But he can sing every lament. When his batteries run out he sits at the window and sings the whole record to the stars. Last time I was in Alice I bought him a bag of batteries. He has his music and a copy of Dante's *Purgatory* that a mission priest gave him thirty years ago. Those and the desert.'

Thompson stared wistfully into the rubying fire. 'You know, there are times in this life when I think if a man was careful like him—limited himself to what was necessary—well—he could almost be happy.'

I wondered what personal tragedy lay behind a comment like that. A broken marriage. A lost child. Perhaps it was the tensions I had read artistic life placed on one's family. Finally, I thought it better not to ask.

'How does Warragul come to be here?'

'Years ago a boxing troupe came through looking for fighters. Warragul landed with the troupe but never left. He told me he just likes the lay of the country.' I looked over Thompson shoulder into the enormous dark. 'Anyway,' he said. 'I told Warragul you might go see him tomorrow.'

Old Warragul's humpy was a box of rotting boards and corrugated iron. A single paneless window faced the Tanami. The opposite wall of the humpy sat at the brink of the bone-dry course these people had memory or audacity or hope enough to call a creek.

A very short and scrawny man with a face blacker than night stood at the door when I got out of my Land Cruiser. At the first rasp of his voice I could smell he had been drinking. It was eight o'clock in the morning.

There was one chair, a table and a thin, sour mattress inside. The Palestrina cassette and two fingers of rum in a square bottle sat on the table beside *Purgatory* and the Bible.

Where every other man and woman at Gurindji had been cagily silent, Old Warrugul talked like a fountain. And suddenly everything Thompson had told me about the old man sounded like exaggeration.

'Can't a black man die in peace, boss . . . I dunno what country Ned Miriwoong took . . . E came ere with a boxing show . . . E spoke a language that sounded like birds . . . the angin tree . . . an old ghost gum . . . Did the boy ang imself then? . . . Murdered you say! . . . Well you're the whitefella . . . And you wanna take me and show me the tree do ya?'

I put Warragul in the cruiser and had him direct me to the ghost gum. I knew from reports that the tree was three miles west of Gurindji. I showed Warragul my GPS. I told him it was a map of the whole country, of the world. He looked at it briefly and nodded.

'So why ya need me to find a tree for ya, boss?'

'It doesn't mark trees.'

We came to the ghost gum: a flare of white against red earth and Prussian blue sky. There were car tracks west of the tree. Also a clean nick in the trunk.

'A bullet?'

Warragul shrugged his shoulders. 'Ya'd av to find it to be sure, boss.'

I looked across the hopeless red earth to the horizon.

'Maybe we'll av a look on ya letric map.'

I thought he was making fun of me, but no smile broke upon his face.

'Do you know what happened here, Warragul?'

'Bloody hot out ere now, boss. Let's go back, eh?'

'You know, you can go to jail for withholding information.'

'Jail!' The old man laughed. 'I bin before. I walked right outa there.'

I sighed and imagined the kind of picketed yard he might have escaped from decades ago, when aborigines were still mustered to be educated or put to work.

'Perhaps we'll talk later. Perhaps tonight.'

'Not unless ya wanna get stuck in me humpy.' He squinted painfully at the blank sky. 'Dust storm comin, boss.'

I tried to see a variant shade of blue on the horizon. I took note of the wind; the same wind, I thought, that had blown from the west since I arrived.

'I might bring you a bottle,' I said. 'Next time—tonight or tomorrow—I'll bring a bottle and we'll talk.

The old man's eyes fell to the dirt.

'Alright, boss.'

The window only offered a metre of vision that night in

the hut with Thompson. The landscape was swallowed by red dust.

'How does he know?'

Thompson shrugged.

'I doubt he'd be able to tell you, any more than you'd be able to explain how you recognise the melody of a song.'

I told Thompson that weather forecasting aside I was a little underwhelmed by Old Warragul:

'He stank of drink.'

I suggested the drinking might have been for my benefit. Warragul would not have been the first aborigine to discover that pretence to alcoholism is a fine ruse in a country that has already made up its mind on that score.

Thompson shook his head.

'It's a genuine vice. Picked up in one reserve or another I suppose.'

'He told me he doesn't have to talk to me. He thinks he could walk out of a jail as easily as the door of his humpy.' I shook my head. 'If only he knew.'

'But he's right after a fashion,' said Thompson. 'He means the country is in his mind. Like a sort of poetic map: like that book of Dante's he reads. Wherever he was put, he'd just close his eyes and get on his knees and sing his way into it. His map covers country he's walked and country he's never even seen. He doesn't know how much country, or time. When he sings he takes water side by side with men who drank at creeks thousands of years ago. So he defies Heraclitus's aphorism about never stepping in the same river twice. The song belongs to a different dialect to what's spoken here though. I reckon Old Warragul might be eighty. Given the fact he's happy to live at Gurindji amidst a foreign tongue, he's likely the last man on earth who speaks — whatever his language is. The last man on earth who knows his song.'

Thompson turned on an electric light as the dust and setting sun conspired to darkness.

'But he's boasting, too.' I said. 'You know how often they kill themselves in jail.'

'Or are killed,' said Thompson wryly. 'Still, I imagine the amount of whisky he drinks erodes the edges of his country.'

'Where does he get it?'

'Truck drivers. Louts. People who bring it on charter planes.'

'There doesn't seem to be enough money out here to make it worthwhile.'

'From time to time there's an influx of cash. But it vanishes just as quickly as it comes.

Late that night a vehicle pulled into Gurindji. Thompson and I were woken by the headlights in our window and the frantic gurgle of aboriginal voices. By the time I had my boots on and walked down the stairs the truck was gone. I watched its taillights glide across the desert.

I went to the wire-bearded elder.

'Who was that?'

'No one, boss.' His red eyes blinked. 'E lookin fa Billiluna. Furder up da track.'

The next day I returned to Old Warragul's humpy. No one was home. I took a fold-out chair from my cruiser and sat waiting till evening.

When he arrived Old Warragul told me he had been walkabout:

'To get me spirit in order'.

The blue dusk settled over us and we sat with a bottle of whisky and a candle.

The old man's eyes began to cloud with the drink. His shoulders sank.

'Why you whitefellas care anyway? Say it wasn suicide. So one blackfella kill another blackfella. We blackfellas' heads are fulla spooks. We might do anythin — for any reason. Wass dat gotta do wit any whitefella?'

'It has to do with the laws of the country,' I said.

'The laws a the country,' the old man laughed. His voice became raspier and his eyes redder as he drank. 'There are older laws than what you call the laws a the country, boss.'

'I know them.' I had read books on tribal law at university.

'Do ya? Av ya read this?'

He tapped his rotten-nailed finger on *Purgatory*.

'I'm not a religious man, nor much of a reader of old poetry.'

'You don't av ta be slidin on ya belly ta get bitten by a snake! The old laws'll find ya, boss. It don't matter if ya believe in em.' He took another sip of whisky. I picked up the Dante volume and chanced upon the line: *My brother, we are all citizens of the one city*.

'Do you know what I think, Warragul? I think you know exactly what happened to Ned Miriwoong. I think everyone at Gurindji knows, even Thompson the painter; that he sent me to talk to you because you're the craftiest bloke here, the best storyteller — because he was afraid the people at Gurindji were such bad liars they'd slip something. I think that on the night I came, whoever was responsible went, or was sent, walkabout — out there!'

I said this pointing through the window to the desert.

I should have expected the smile that wrinkled the old man's face.

'If e was sent out there and asn bin back since you got ere, boss, then e's dead . . . that's if there was anyone to send.'

Little by little the liquor was loosening the truth from Warragul's tongue.

'He might not be dead if he knows where to find water.'

'Not much water out there, boss.'

'But you know where to find it. You might have been out there finding it for him today.' I sighed. 'Listen Warragul. I think Ned Miriwoong was killed over drugs, or drink, or even petrol. A deal gone wrong. A theft. A lie. Something trivial like that. A car pulled up last night at Gurindji and then vanished. I think it was a booze runner. Likely someone who has something to do with this business. How does that sound?'

Warragul seemed properly drunk now, after only one tin cup of whisky. His wrinkled skin was suddenly pulled tight across his cheekbones. He sat in silence I thought he might never break.

'You know what I reckon?' he rasped. His eyes were the colour of the candle flame he stared at. 'What I know? The death is the end of an old dispute between two of the desert clans. One of them—I don't remember which—joined up with the police. Under orders or outa malevolence they blocked a walkin track to water. The other clan got sick from bad water. Many died.'

'When was that?'

The old man looked out at the stars.

'Undred years ago.'

'One hundred years!'

'Undred years isn a long time to a desert, boss . . . and blackfellas av minds made outa sand.'

I took a drink of whisky.

'Revenge isn't how we do things in the 21st Century.

'The 21st Century got nothin to do with this country, boss.'

But Old Warragul realised I would not quit. I told him if he did not speak, I would drive on to Billiluna, and perhaps I would find someone there who would.

'Well, what if I did see somethin? What if I was gone walkabout and saw somethin I never meant to? Saw a man who mighta done it. What would that mean?'

'It would mean you and me would go looking for a murderer. He's out there isn't he? I knew it. We'll leave tomorrow. The only good water is to the north, toward the Kimberly. He's gone that way, hasn't he? Don't worry if he's made threats, I'll protect you, Warragul.'

The old man nodded and poured another cup of whisky.

That night in the plywood hut Thompson asked me for a drink, I believe it was only to confirm his suspicion, to see that I was short one bottle. He glared at me and switched off the light.

But the next day he lent me his pony for a packhorse and I set out northwest with Warragul, my GPS, and provisions enough to last a fortnight.

We walked through infernal heat, monotonous termite mounds and across dunes of Spinifex on an awful gibber plain. But the worst was following the trail of a man, who was perhaps merely a figment of my imagination; a trail that my tracker nonetheless now claimed he had picked up. And Warragul sang. He sang the song that I supposed was the map Thompson had told me about back at Gurindji.

At night Warragul dug down into soaks below creek beds to replenish a little of what we had drunk in the day. He collected grubs to roast from the rare bloodwood trees we camped beneath.

After two days he claimed to have seen the man we were looking for on the horizon. The following day, and the day after that, the same. But he always saw him at dusk, when my eyes failed me. I put on my glasses and squinted in the direction he pointed but saw nothing.

When the sun rose Warragul would show me tracks that came from nowhere and went nowhere. The tracks' extremes were blown away by the wind, as though the wind hand spilled along narrow channels, just as water runs in that country after rain. Warragul told me the winds out here were known to behave that way due to rock outcrops and rapid drops and peaks in temperature. The tracks seemed to fit our quarry: a ghost who might tread on the sand only when he chose.

I woke in the middle of one night to find Warragul gone. I called his name and got no answer. He returned out of the dark an hour later with a handful of small birds eggs.

'Breakfast,' he said.

'Don't you dare leave me.'

I tried to go back to sleep.

In the middle of the fifth day we found a well. My GPS marked the position, but not the nature of the country we stood in. We must have been on the fringes of some fenceless old cattle station. Warragul shook his head at the well.

'No good, boss.' Bad spirits in dat water. Man killed ere one time.'

'When?'

He looked up at the cloudless blue sky and across the desert.

'Two undred years ago.'

I spat and stared at him.

'There were no white men to dig wells in this country even a hundred years ago.'

I dropped a metal bucket down five metres and drew up water that was too sulphurous to swallow.

Further along we found another well.

'This one good, boss. Old stockman fell off is orse ere. Good fella. His ghost keep the water runnin.'

I laughed when the bucket came up with water, brown but fresh. I took a handful to my mouth and nodded and Warragul smiled.

'How do you know?'

'Old song,' he said.

But shortly after, Warragul stood on a patch of stony red earth and turned around and around, squinting hopelessly into every horizon like a caricature of lostness.

'Maybe we should walk back a way, boss.'

'How far?'

He measured the distance between the sun and the earth with his fingers.

'Arf a day.'

I winced. But I was determined not to be broken, even if we were chasing a phantom.

And all the while Warragul sang. Except for those times he stopped still and listened.

'You ear that, boss?'

I think his hearing was the one sense he did not wholly trust. I heard it too, a faint, dull roar, ahead of us and to the west. I thought it was a car engine. But then the sound would die in the wind.

That night Warragul sang by the campfire, that strange, guttural melisma that at times sounded like medieval chant. Without a break he glided into Palestrina's first Lament of Jeremiah. I was trying to revive my GPS that had malfunctioned and gave me only a blank screen.

'Tell me about the old dispute,' I said.

Warragul broke off his song.

'We're nearly in the place,' he said. 'Purnululu some call it. Till a few years ago no whitefella'd ever seen it. It's an ancient border between the desert-livin Jaru in the east and the savannah-livin Kija in the west. Fulla old burial grounds, fireplaces, sacred country. It belongs to the Kija—one clan of em—but the Jaru—one clan of em—had holy walkin rights. Then one drought time the Kija stopped the Jaru goin in there for water. Twelve Jaru died. So the Jaru killed twelve Kija. But the Kija elder wanted to see the twelve Jaru dead of thirst. The Jaru showed im only eleven. One's body'd bin takin by the flood God made at last to quench the Jaru where they camped at the border. But the Kija wouldn believe it. A Kija warrior crossed the border and crept into the Jaru camp at night and killed a Jaru. The night after that, a Jaru killed a Kija . . .'

'That's different from the story you told me back at Gurindji.'

'The story's stronger in this country.'

'Where's your country,'

He whirled his finger in the air in a way that could have meant here, a hundred miles away or the stars. He sipped his tea and spoke mysteriously: 'When I was your age, boss, govament employed me to find artesian water.

It was far east of ere. Me and this other whitefella. E got two shillins a map. I got blankets and whisky and a hatchet.' He looked up at the stars. 'I'm losin my country. But I won't loose much more of it.'

In the night I dreamt I heard a vehicle. I woke and saw Warragul sitting wide awake and watching me across the coals of the fire.

The next day we walked over sand and rock into a dream. A spine of coloured sandstone rose out of the desert like an abandoned city. We walked into a slot in the rock. The horrid call of a crow echoed down the gorge, but Old Warragul's song rang louder.

'This is where he'll be, boss.'

We followed creeks and climbed over boulders; we walked through tunnels into amphitheatres where tea-coloured waterholes reflected the sky and conglomerate cliffs. This sculptured city of stone bore witness to the movement of vast and ancient waters.

We walked into dark passageways that turned and turned like arcades in a medieval town. Light bent around the corners, leading us on. Fairy wrens and finches flew between the walls and their chirping rang like strange bells. I took out my revolver. I waited for a blow to come, either from Warragul or that ghost I might merely have dreamed.

At midday, with the sun directly above, all the dark recesses of the place were lit.

Warragul looked down at our feet, at definite tracks.

'E's bin ere, alright, boss.'

But in an hour of searching there was no sign of him.

We sat by a waterhole with the pony tethered to a solitary bloodwood. I was as tired as I had ever been. I knew we could not go on; I was defeated. I watched dragonflies skipping across the water while Warragul sang.

I heard a vehicle.

Warragul's eyes lit up. He stood and began to sing as loudly as ever and the song rebounded off the stone walls like the music of a great dark choir. I followed his hunched frame between rocks and out into the open and saw a blonde-haired man and a part-aboriginal boy in a battered yellow cruiser. I saw a third man stand up in the tray with a rifle. Old Warragul held up his fists and glared at the men in a warrior's stance and before I could fire a shot the man in the back of the truck had shot Warragul through the heart. He slumped bleeding onto the broken sandstone. I fired and took out one of the truck's mirrors. Another blast from the rifle had me ducking behind a rock wall. I got my eye and hand around the edge of the rock and fired and hit the shoulder of the boy in the tray. The truck turned around and another shot cracked from the passenger window sending me back behind the wall. I knelt low and fired the revolver empty, but the truck was gone out of range.

I picked Old Warragul up from where he lay face down, blood streaming out of the wound in his chest. I heard footsteps behind me and then from out of the dark of a gallery I saw the flash of white eyes. A crying boy came and supported Warragul's head. The old man smiled at the boy before he died.

'Who are you?' I said.

'His nephew. Ned Miriwoong.'

We buried Old Warragul under shards of sandstone in a deep cave. We untethered the pony and set off back to Gurindji.

On the journey I discovered the boy was Warragul's pupil. He was learning Warragul's song . . .

'But the booze runners were killin the old bloke.' Tears stained the boy's face while he spoke. 'I told em to keep away. They threatened im. So next time a man came to sell drink at Gurindji, at the ghost gum where they always done the deal, I shot im.'

The man was insignificant: another poor aborigine; a mule working for a man in Alice.

'After I shot that bloke I found Warragul makin his way to the tree for is liquor.'

Then, the boy told me, the two of them took a rope out of the unknown man's car and tied it around his neck and lifted him up onto the tree. Ned drove the car miles into the desert and he and Warragul walked back to Gurindji. They had the painter take the grisly photograph I had seen in reports in Darwin. Soon after, they buried the body in a decades-dry water course, so the police would not discover the flesh wound. And then all Gurindji had said that the local boy Ned Miriwoong was dead and buried.

'When e never come back, the booze runners musta figured their bloke was dead, too. Else went walkabout after killin a local boy. Blood for blood. Either way, we reckoned they'd never come lookin for im. But then you—'

'Warragul told me it was an old border dispute. Over water.'

The boy shook his head.

On that awful walk back I realised Old Warragul had sung out loud to give our position, to make sure the boy would never stumble into us, while he kept close to the old man who was his means of survival out there. And, of course, those mysterious foot tracks were made by the old man in the nights when I was asleep, the tracks back to camp he brushed away with bloodwood switches. It seems more foolish here at a lamp-lit writing desk than it did on that ancient plain to have believed the wind could be so deliberate.

At Gurindji I told Thompson what had happened. For a time, he only sat on the stairs of our hut and smoked. Then he came back inside.

'Some corrupted bastard from around here must have got wind of you. Maybe even tracked you for a way. Likely whoever pulled up here in that truck the other night.'

'But how does a truck appear with armed men in the middle of the desert coming from the opposite direction.'

Thompson unfolded a map and pointed.

'There are roads near where you walked. Old and bad roads, but still roads. Whoever found out what you were doing must have radioed through to men in the Kija country to the north. Got someone to meet you. There are gangs of them.'

'Radioed through and said what?'

'That a cop was using a tracker to find something out about the Ned Miriwoong case. They probably thought you were going after their man—the one who's buried in the desert.'

'I wouldn't have thought they'd care.'

'Not about his life. Only his propensity to talk.' Thompson stared out the window.

I glanced at one of my whisky bottles in the corner of the hut.

I told Thompson what Warragul had told me about the ancient border dispute between the Jaru and the Kija, about the water.

'I guess it was just a scrap of old song he confused with reality,' I said.

'And yet,' said Thompson. 'It has been over water. Blood and alcohol.'

I raised my eyebrows.

'And perhaps now the last missing Jaru has been found dead.'

'Yes,' Thompson sighed. 'For God's sake give me a drink.'

I opened a bottle.

'Are you going to take the boy in? After all, he's killed a man — whoever that poor bastard is they buried out there.'

I stood up and went to the door and saw the boy standing by the fire with a spindly, grey-headed woman.

'Do you think he could walk out of a jail like Warragul?'

'Perhaps he knows part of Warragul's way out. But no. He wouldn't last long behind bars. One way or another it'd kill him.'

I sighed and sat down on the stairs.

That night I dreamt of a landscape of dry mountains that were no more permanent than a field of desert wildflowers, than dust motes, than — some-illogical-how — the arrangements of stars. It was my job to map the land. I was the boy they had hired for blankets, whisky and hatchets for the work, but it was like trying to map the surface of the ocean.

I headed back to Alice Springs alone the next day.

By the Aral Sea

I T WAS SUMMER VACATION. I had escaped my university in Beijing and taken the Trans-Siberian Railway across north-western China and then a series of buses to the Aral Sea. The town the bus pulled into was once a coastal town. Now the water had withdrawn beyond the western horizon. Massive merchant ships fell over in the sandy channels that were dredged for them before the water disappeared. White camels walked about the ships' rusted hulls. And the town, along with concrete quay and dock, sat in the midst of a blowing desert. I do not remember the name of the town; I wrote it in a notebook that I left on a Russian train.

I walked door to door offering money till someone took me in: a man of about forty with fierce green eyes set in a typically dark Central Asian face. I have forgotten his name; I will call him Adarburzin, which is a common enough name in that country. The house was made of wood and the wallboards were decorated with arabesques of blue, red and green. There was even a courtyard that housed a malnourished cow.

I told the man how beautiful I thought his house was. He waved the suggestion away as though it were an insult.

Like all Central Asian villagers, Adarburzin desired an apartment in an awful soviet building in a grey capital.

His wife was dead five years. His teenage daughter

served tea, then sang and played on an instrument that looked like a very long-handled lute, with three strings and a small teardrop soundbox. I wrote the name of the instrument in the same notebook that now travels, obscured beneath seats, through indistinguishable cities and unmemorable plains between Beijing and Siberia.

'It's one thousand years old. A nomad instrument,' said Marjan when I asked. Her name I have not forgotten. We spoke Russian, her second language. I had taken my first lessons from a phrase book on the train, so our conversation was very simple

'Two thousand years,' her father corrected.

She played and sang again. I have never heard such a song: elegantly rising toward a pitch that was finally out of reach, then falling in order to rise again. Her song seemed as ancient and strange as the shepherds that moved small flocks about here without any visible grass or fresh water; as sad as the vanished sea and poisonous wind. She told me the lyrics were taken from Hilâli, a classical poet of Islam. I shuddered when she put the instrument away in her room and I saw a poster of an American pop singer pinned to the wall.

'The water is still receding,' said Adarburzin. He told me the water went so fast there were days that fish got stranded. Then fisherman like himself shovelled them up and there were too many for the factories. But now there were not nearly enough and most of the factories were closed.

Adarburzin told me how the Amu Darya and Syr Darya rivers feed the Aral Sea when there is rain on Mount Imeon and when the snow melts in the Himalayas. 'But today,' he said, 'what is left is all salt and pesticides'—the last word he found for me in my dictionary. He sighed painfully and shook his head. 'The Soviet's cotton is to blame. They took the river water. Then every farm and orchard and garden was taken. If you didn't farm cotton you were sent to prison.'

Now the bulldozers that dug the irrigation canals were out there rusting with everything else.

Adarburzin said he had to drive many hours to the western basin, else the same distance to fish the northern lakes, else he fished the Syr Darya now. And he did not have a license anymore.

'And the fishing is not good.'

Mostly he sold scrap metal that he took from the stranded ships. But tomorrow he would take me fishing.

We slept on camelhair mats on the wooden floor.

The Syr Darya was a mirror of the sky. Marjan fished with us. I asked Adarburzin if his daughter often accompanied him. 'Very often,' he said.

She spent the day smiling benevolently at my attempts to cast and retrieve her father's nets, often helping. I watched her work and wondered at the strength of her delicate frame and thought how Adarburzin had lost nothing in not having a son. I realised I had seen very few young men in the region.

Adarburzin nodded in answer to my observation. 'Many go to the cities,' he said. 'Many to the army. Some are sick from working on the sea.'

He told me Marjan was seventeen, though she looked barely fifteen to me. And this Central Asian life is hard on girls, on their faces and hands. Girls of twenty have sun and wind-burnt skin that is resplendent and beautiful but makes them look ten years older. I did not guess what reason the man had to lie.

The next day we drove a rusted car owned by Adarburzin

and his brother. We drove to a western village where the Aral Sea had not receded, to visit their mother's family. Poisoned as it was, I have never seen such a strangely beautiful body of water. Red flowers littered the shore, and all through the day and night the sea changed colour. Cobalt in the morning, turquoise at dusk, midnight green at twilight.

At twilight Marjan and I walked along the shore. Earlier in the day her father had taken me aside, noting how we enjoyed each other's company. He had said: 'My daughter is yours if you will keep her. Marry her. Take her to your home!' I told him it was impossible. Certainly, it was impossible. I was twenty-seven; she was likely no more than fifteen. She did not have a certificate to prove her birth, much less a passport. She could not speak English.

'She is kind,' her father said, 'and good with her hands. She can walk many miles in a day. She is prayerful. She can fish and make good tea and she can sing.'

I sighed. I did not tell him that none of those things were valued in my city home; the kind of place these people fashion dreams about. It was one of those rare occasions when I wished my home was not my home. I wished I was a citizen of somewhere else. Somewhere simpler. Even here, with all its tragedy.

I stepped with Marjan along the shore. The blue water lapped about our feet. Her dark hair was wrapped in a red scarf. She half-hummed, half-sang a Tajik folk song. She was happy, perhaps dreaming she was my wife. I was dreaming that. She looked up at me and smiled and her eyes twinkled beneath the red scarf. And all at once I imagined her in a Brisbane social security office, in a cheap women's business suit, filling out a benefit claim form with an official glaring superiorly across the desk at her. No, I thought. I would not take you away from here if it were as easy as boarding a boat.

I looked at her bare feet. The bottom of her dress was wet and wrapped around her legs. An anklet flashed in the moonlight. The anklet, she had told me that day, belonged to her great great grandmother. I had stopped myself from voicing stupid surprise that it had never gone out of fashion. I looked in her dark eyes then turned away to the ever-vanishing water.

'Why are you sad?' she asked.

'For the sea. For what has gone away and is not coming back.'

'Yes. It is very sad.'

'I left the following day for Tashkent.'

Music for Airports

I T WAS SIX O CLOCK and autumn and the diplomat watched the flare at the oil refinery gather brightness against the dusk. Between the window and the refinery was a nebulous landscape of paperbarks and mangroves that made no loud demand on the eye. Above the trees was a stream of dark flecks. Roughly a dozen birds.

'Waders,' said a cleaner who had noticed the diplomat looking out the window. 'Godwits and Eastern Curlews.'

The cleaner spoke with an uncommon foreign accent. He smiled wrinkles into his dark skin and took off his cap to reveal a sweat-dampened crop of short oriental-black hair.

The diplomat asked the cleaner where he was from.

'Those birds are going to my home,' the man said. 'Irkutsk. On Lake Baikal. They leave with the first breath of cold from the south. I watch them everyday in May. Fewer each year.' The cleaner shook his head. 'They don't live where the city goes.' He smiled: 'My mother used to say they carried souls to the southern heaven. They fly hundreds of miles overnight into fierce winds. No one knows how they find their way.'

The cleaner took up his mop and bucket and walked away and the diplomat closed his eyes and lay back in his chair.

The diplomat wondered how the cleaner could identify the birds at this distance. He doubted he could.

Ambient muzak flowed around him and the soft light inside the transit lounge overcame the light outside. The landscape dissolved and the transit lounge window became a mirror and the diplomat stared at his own face. He thought about the birds that were lost in the dark. A Boeing 737 turned silently onto the runway and its wingtip-strobes beat a line along the tarmac. With his index finger he lifted the plane into the sky.

The darkness was already in the east offshore. Twelve curlew stepped along the shoreline below pearl white clouds and the last ebb of twilight. The tide was leaving. A bird's long beak retrieved a bloodworm from the sand. The bird lifted its wings and felt cold air rush beneath. The bird's awkward-long legs rose above the sand and then the bird—three others—the twelve rose into the teeth of the wind and all at once the wind that came from the direction in which they did not ever go further than here was their wind. The stars had been arranging themselves for some nights into the patterns the birds recognised and tonight the stars had arrived as the wind had arrived and made a potent call and each bird gave a call to the others and they turned with the wind and flew for two bright northern stars they knew by wordless name.

The diplomat landed in Narita the next morning and in the second month of spring. A warm shower was falling. Airport workers hurried across the tarmac to the plane in bright yellow raincoats. The airport was filled with chiming and humming electrical sounds. The diplomat felt the unease of the flight fall off him.

He preferred Narita airport to all the airports of the world. Though you did not know the language, it was impossible to put a foot wrong here. Once inside there was no confusion, no clamour. At every turn a pretty Japanese girl with good English—some with French and

German and Chinese—would smile and direct you with a gesture toward customs. Should he marry one day he might choose one of these women who worked at the airport. He wondered how a traveller would go about making an acquaintance. He walked by a smiling girl with perfect skin who stood against an enormous pane of glass. Perhaps he had looked lost as he turned to the window. The young woman extended her hand.

'This way please, sir.'

He nodded and thanked her. He wondered what kind of wife she would make. If she would be obsequious as she seemed, as the myth had it, forever. Or were there hidden depths?

He had slept on the plane so he was not tired and after checking into the Hotel Nikko he took a bus and then a train into Narita city. The train rolled through a landscape dominated by aerials, power lines, and clusters of houses that seemed made out of paper. He was struck, as ever, by the Tokyo satellite's quaint, plastic charm, its orderly streets.

He got off at the centre of town. The rain had become heavy. He bought a blue umbrella. He consulted the map from the hotel. The rain disguised the streets and troubled his memory. He wanted to find an okonomiyaki bar he had eaten at six months ago, but the commercial and entertainment district he walked thinned into residences. He arrived at a street whose shops were interspersed with the paper houses and all appeared closed. He knocked on a door that bore a wooden tablet with red writing that he supposed meant welcome.

A middle-aged woman in formal kimono answered.

'*Hayai ne!*' she declared. The diplomat smiled bemusedly and the woman repeated the word 'early' in English.

He looked at his watch. He thought eleven o'clock was a reasonable time for lunch.

The woman led him into a room that did not bear the normal marks of a public dining room. Two additional ladies appeared: one middle-aged and wearing an apron, the other a girl of twenty or so who looked sleepy and a little dishevelled, as though she had been woken. The diplomat made it understood he wished to eat. The women urged him to sit down at a low and chair-less table. They presented him with tea but no menu and between his few words of Japanese and theirs of English an order for udon noodle soup was taken from a very limited selection of dishes. The three women seemed bored and chatted to each other around a small kotatsu and, very discreetly, watched him eat. At the end of the meal he paid a nominal sum, discussed and agreed on by the two older women.

'Is that all?' said the woman who had answered the door.

'The soup was enough for two.'

He asked the woman to point to the place he was on his map. She did so with no great politeness.

The diplomat walked back to the centre of town. He spent the afternoon reading an airport thriller and watching his fellow over-nighting commuters take photographs of one another in front of a Buddhist temple. In the thriller the entire civilized world stood to be lost but, at last, was saved along with all the characters you cared about.

Neon lights blinked on and the little restaurants and bars lit their lanterns and he walked back to central station. A single night on leave in a Far Eastern city, he thought, is worth a week's holiday in Europe or South East Asia. Somehow the bustle of the great oriental metropolises never affected you personally. The bustle was part of something you were not involved in; you could let it wash around you, like waves in a gentle sea.

Laughter trickled along the narrow alleyways and down from windows. He wondered if the lantern-lit windows were hostess bars. He would feel out of place walking into one of those alone, though that was what they were designed for — the unaccompanied and the lonely. He hailed a bus and watched a blue-suited salary man pushing unnecessarily close to a pair of schoolgirls in the aisle.

Every room, every floor of the hotel Nikko was comfortingly identical. There was a sense of reliving a pleasant time in your past whenever you stayed there. All that varied was the view from the windows. Tonight, the diplomat's window took in the blinking satellite city and an anomalous corner of open landscape: an intensely green field. He saw a spray of dark cross the dusk above the field. He smiled. Birds seemed to be following him. He recalled the birds in another season and hemisphere twenty-four hours ago.

The room's silence was broken by a telephone call.

The voice on the line belonged to a Chinese. The voice hurried and stumbled. The diplomat heard his own name.

'Australian Foreign Affairs?' queried the Chinaman.

Broadly speaking. But he did not work for the department anymore. A year ago he worked in immigration at the embassy in Beijing. Now he was a member of the Queensland China Council, an advisor on trade and investment.

'Who am I speaking to?'

'My name is Yuan, Sir. I'm calling from Hohot.'

The diplomat pictured that freezing, windswept city and his interest in the caller grew.

'You will be in Beijing tomorrow?' said Mr. Yuan.

For an excited moment the diplomat thought his life was about to be touched by an airport novel — perhaps he would be warned of a plot on his life: a planned hijack of tomorrow's flight by terrorists. But that was ridiculous. His purpose in China was merely to shake hands and formalise the delivery of some new rights for Chinese Scientists: a kind of biodiversity lease he barely understood the nature of, a kickback for favourable treatment given to Australian companies investing in China. He was not a part of the process at any but the most superficial level. He was, in the jargon, a mannequin. In honest and whiskied hours he admitted with a little regret that all his assignments were like this. There seemed no harm in telling anyone the truth about being in Beijing tomorrow.

'I work for an international NGO.' said Yuan. He gave a name and an acronym that the diplomat had never heard of.

'There is a man in this province who has received summary trial and is facing execution in as little as forty-eight hours. He has lived in Australia most of his life.'

'All your trials are summary. What has he done?'

'Trafficked opium.'

'Through Hohot?'

'Intending Siberia. It is a backdoor to Europe.'

'A long and rugged back door.'

'But with few meaningful border crossings before Poland.'

'What has this got to do with me?'

'His Chinese name in Lin Zhuang, but you should call him Leo. He went by that name in your country.'

'If this man's a citizen you should be talking to the embassy.'

'He is not a citizen. He lived in Australia most of his life, with his brother who is also not a citizen. And perhaps you know, Sir, how the embassy of your country operates here.'

He did know: a policy of compliance whenever possible. He had discovered that when he was arrested in China, as a student, for trying to protect a girl from a man's unwanted advances. The consulate washed their hands of him. He had spent an entire night with police who tried to extort a large bribe before letting him go with a couple of slaps across the face and what cash was in his pockets.

'Why have you called me?'

'We are contacting others—but you have contacts, both here and in your country. You are in the Department of Foreign Affairs,' the man erred again. 'Two things are essential: we need someone to make the journey here to Hohot to visit Lin Zhuang, and we need his application for citizenship of your country to be approved.'

'Has he applied?'

'The last time was a year ago. His first application was lost. You see, he has no money. He applies on grounds of refugee status and attachment to the country.'

The diplomat knew those were the worst grounds.

'Zhuang's last application is still being processed. We hope it's still valid. We want you to use your influence. You know that foreigners cannot be executed in China.'

That was true. But did the man on the line have any idea of the machinery that would need to be altered to achieve his end? Does a man simply start telephoning high-ranking people and newspaper editors in bed? Heroes did in airport novels. He asked himself what benefit there would be for party politicians in pulling foreign criminals off the scaffold because they claimed a love of the country.

'Do you really think Australians will sympathise with

a man with a foreign name and a foreign passport caught trafficking drugs in a place they've never heard of?'

'Lin Zhuang is not a criminal. He is a victim of circumstance. You will see. We must arrange a meeting tomorrow in Beijing, when you are free.'

'I'm sorry, but I won't be free anytime tomorrow. The next day, perhaps.'

'The next day is no good. Tomorrow.'

'I can't promise you that. Understand, Mr. Yuan, as unsympathetic as I am with your country's laws, for all we know it was my government's police who informed on the boy and had him arrested offshore. You know how it is in the present mood—global intelligence sharing and all that.'

'We call it outsourcing the death penalty.'

The diplomat sighed.

'Lin Zhuang loves birds,' said Yuan. 'We gave him a notebook to write letters, but after his brother he did not have anyone else to write to. Instead he draws pictures of birds in his cell.' There was a long pause. 'I'm sorry,' said Yuan. 'That is a personal thing. That is irrelevant.'

It was. Yet, the diplomat was affected by it.

'Fax your phone number and what information you have to the hotel tonight. Send nothing to the hotel in Beijing. I'll contact you. I'm not frightened for myself, obviously, but it's just more trouble than it's worth. I'll collect what you send in the morning. If I feel there's any benefit in our meeting, then we will.'

When the call was ended the diplomat looked out the window at that one patch of true dark, the field, unmolested by Narita's lights. He was too excited now for the silence of the room, it demanded too much patience. He turned on the television. He flicked through the free-to-air Japanese stations, the American movies, the Japanese pornography channel . . .

The lights of Irian Jaya and then the sun rose on water. The birds had flown into a contrary wind for hours in the dark and now they looked for somewhere to land.

A shower came and then heavier rain and the birds could not see but by the soundless voice that whispered to them. The voice was always there and only in the big over-lit and noisy cities did it become dim. A speck on the northern horizon became an oil rig. The rig's electric lights burned against a grey sky. The birds landed and fluffed and plumed their feathers. A few men stood on the piled deck in the rain. One man shooed them for boredom and the birds took turns in flying up above the deck and landing again and eventually the man grew tired and left the birds alone.

The diplomat came from breakfast into the lobby and the concierge hurried to him with a large yellow envelope.

'A fax for you, sir.'

He went to the hotel garden and took out the contents of the envelope: a letter from the man called Yuan along with a twelve page dossier, the case file of Lin Zhuang, Mongolian–Chinese 'Australian' arrested and convicted as a drug mule.

Lin Zhuang faced the firing squad. He had lived in Australia for eleven years since his father, now dead, had been arrested as a dissident. He had taken first year science at James Cook University in Cairns, but was forced to withdraw due to lack of money. He moved to Brisbane, to Moreton Bay, where he and his brother cleaned local business houses at night. Through the day he sketched birds – that irrelevant point again. Lin Zhuang had hoped to save enough money to return to university and become an ornithological artist. According to the NGO's report he smuggled the drugs in an attempt to pay off a debt run up by his brother with a gang. He had acted only in order to prevent his brother's murder. There was a copy of a letter by an Australian legal aid lawyer who was working without pay. The lawyer wanted Lin Zhuang tried in Australia. It was only a bureaucratic delay, he argued, that denied him citizenship. Lin Zhuang had been picked up in Hohot. He had gone there as he knew the people and the language, though he had left the place as a child.

The diplomat wondered why Lin Zhuang did not make the journey down through South-East Asia. He supposed once in Europe getting caught would not have been so deadly an affair. Yet caught in Asia the boy was. Perhaps Europe was the drop off point. The case file did not say. It was not well written. Poor English. Why not take a plane? Perhaps Lin Zhuang knew he was being tailed. Perhaps he wanted to avoid airport customs.

'Poor fool.'

The diplomat waited in the hotel garden. A white plastic chair, left over from a wedding reception the night before, sat isolated on the lawn. There was a poster-board picketed in the lawn advertising wedding packages and their costs in Japanese yen and the corresponding amount in US dollars. Weddings in Japan were becoming popular with foreigners who wanted to shorten their guest lists. The diplomat ran his fingers over a cherry blossom branch and in the pale blue sky were birds. Roughly a dozen flying north. He wondered if these were an advance guard of the birds he had seen through the airport window two nights ago.

The birds had flown eighteen hours without rest and were landed on the south face of a mountain. A half-dozen men stood carrying rifles on their shoulders on a dirt track. The birds kept their distance. A square field of pink flowers had grown up on the mountain since the birds were last here. Every other year in this season the field was a field of ash below a haze of yellow smoke. The men with rifles stood at the edges of the crop and occasionally switched places. The men were tired with sitting still and one said the harvest was very late and held his palm out to show it had already begun to rain and asked why they had still not gotten word from above. The men looked angry and uncomfortable and one said it was already time to be scoring and burning and to be gone and then there was a loud argument between two of the men and then a gunshot and then one of the men fell dead. The birds were frightened by the shot and flew on to the north.

The plane descended through grey cloud and into Beijing. The diplomat wondered why he was so fond of the city. Much of Beijing was ugly. But the greyness, the apparent uniformity of the people and buildings, became pleasing after a while. It reminded him of Dante's grey Limbo, where the pagan poets and infidel philosophers endure no punishment but the turned face of God, where he imagined he would not be entirely unhappy wandering painlessly, without hope or obligation among the other irretrievable shades; at least, so long as there were women to keep him company and neon lights to make a haze of the dark.

The diplomat attended his meeting in a function room of the Office of Foreign Enterprise in Fengtai District. He shook hands with politicians, other diplomats and scientists. Experience told him some of the latter were actors, there for the benefit of newspaper photographers and television cameras. He asked a simple question of one very pretty lady scientist who could not answer him in any language. In a country so confused with people and names, no one seemed to doubt or believe much in the existence of anyone. The uncommonly tall diplomats were genuine though — graduates from Beijing Foreign Studies University, the school with its secret height and beauty requirements for admission, where he had studied for a semester on scholarship.

He gave a brief interview to the *China Daily* in English, another in rudimentary Mandarin to Chinese network television with the help of a female translator who had been assigned to him. He answered questions thoughtlessly. He knew it did not matter what he said, that even in the unlikely event the interview did make a news program he would end up a flashing face mouthing a sentence fragment beneath the mechanical Mandarin of the newsreader.

Through the morning he had grown to like his translator's face. And her voice made Mandarin sound like peals of tiny bells and intimate whispers. She told him she was a Masters student in international relations. She mentioned something about the possibility of a man picking her up at the end of the day and the diplomat imagined a boyfriend and became jealous. He invited the girl to dinner under the pretence of straightening out some political jargon.

'You will be paid, of course. In addition to the meal.'

She smiled courteously and agreed.

The pretence of work was insupportable and vanished shortly. The pair conversed idly in English at a French café in Beijing World Park. The diplomat was surprised she had never been there before. He felt sure she would appreciate it, seeing she hoped to be in foreign affairs herself one day. They sat in view of a replica Eiffel Tower. The diplomat ordered them toasted baguettes and champagne. A man in Bedouin costume led a camel across the road to be stabled.

'But, of course, you don't really see China from the window of a hotel,' she said.

'You're wrong there. You can tell a lot about a country from its hotels.'

'How?'

'The fancy hotels in Australia don't keep pretty young prostitutes. That tells you something about the distribution of wealth, and government corruption. French hotel employees won't automatically speak English to you. They're reluctant to even when they know it's your language. That tells you something about a nation's sense of itself.'

'What about the chain hotels?'

'Once they were the same everywhere. Now in China they keep prostitutes too.' The diplomat sighed, 'But even then they're sterile places. You never meet anyone you didn't expect to. You get nothing you didn't pay for.'

'You see and hear all the signs of life from my dormitory,' the girl said. 'It backs onto an alley we call *'Conglaibu Shui,* Never Sleeps'. I can sleep through traffic, music and vending, but if I hear a scream or cry it will keep me awake. I wonder is it only a brother pulling his little sister by the hair, or something sinister. I heard one last night—a scream.'

'Did you investigate?'

'How could I? You could search the tenements and hovels all night. And what law would support you even if you did find a father beating a child, or a madam torturing a girl. There is nothing you can do. So it must have been arguing children after all. So, last night, I lay awake until the screaming went away.'

'I've never heard a scream in a hotel room,' the diplomat confessed. 'My rooms are silent.'

The girl smiled politely and looked across the tables

toward three Cantonese businessmen stripping the flesh from a fish with chopsticks. The diplomat realised he was losing her interest.

Spring's dust storms had not yet abated and there were very few people at the park tonight. The storms might rise at any hour. A cold wind blew down the artificial French boulevard. The girl did not want coffee. Suddenly the night seemed unnecessarily prolonged. Some key term or phrase had been spoken, or left unspoken, that meant they would not be intimate, not even friends. They sat at the table together and utterly alone. He asked if she would like to go somewhere else — to a nightclub. But she did not want to. She must return to the university. She did not realise how late it had become.

The birds had flown six and a half thousand kilometres across four national borders and landed in what only a year ago was a wetland and now was a polluted swamp. The river that watered the land was blackened with leaked pollutants; a little further down steam at a concrete wall it stopped altogether. The birds picked around tidal rubbish but found nothing to eat and knew there could be no good rest here. They were very tired. The voice they heard remembered when men were not in this place and perhaps they would go away soon, but a little dark-skinned girl came out of a shanty of rusted iron with a dog's bowl of water and a handful of mussels. She fed the birds and the birds stayed a little longer than they would have.

The diplomat asked for Gordon's gin and tonic water to be sent to the room. In the later stages of drunkenness he looked out the hotel window and thought again about the girl. What had she thought of him? It was near impossible to tell. The Chinese could be so reserved, as reserved as they could be flagrantly rude. He had arrived back too late for the prostitute's nightly visit. He thought about calling for a girl to be sent up, but shortly he was too drunk and tired. He thought how everything was easier with the girls you paid for. With the others there were always complications, misunderstandings, finally unpleasantness. A girl tomorrow night. The suspended pleasure made him happier, made him feel more secure. There were hours at a time he felt utterly lost, and this night had begun to string them together. There were nights he woke from sleep and forgot where he was, what he was doing, once even the name of his home city.

He looked down to the sleepless street and saw a man with a twig-broom in a blue 'comrade's coat' sweeping the road. A half-dozen birds landed on an awning. The street-sweeper threw something from his pocket, a bit of rice or cake crumbs, and the birds floated to his feet. A group of revelling university students sent the birds flapping back into the violet glow of the polluted sky.

The diplomat thought about his flight tomorrow. He checked his ticket. He was very drunk and tired now. Something he had read or dreamt made him imagine something terrible was about to happen . . . but he could not remember what . . . He imagined his plane hijacked by terrorists. If his plane went down a page of a broadsheet might be devoted to him. He would have liked his plane to be hijacked, to crash, so long as he could hover above it. Watch the burning through the glass of a window like the one he looked through now, then go on living.

He looked again to the crowds on the street. Beautiful women. He imagined they were so, though he could not see their faces. Filthy beggars. Mongolian workers. The street sweeper and the birds were gone.

Days later the body of an executed man was taken by six distant relatives and laid in the icy soil of a lakeside cemetery in a wood-and-concrete village outside Irkutsk. The relatives did not mark the grave but for a solitary candle that was extinguished directly the wind rose. A flock of a dozen Eastern Curlew caught an uprush of the same wind that joined them with ten thousand other birds above Lake Baikal. The birds would have peace under the spring sun now, in the wind that blew Beijing and all civilization back from this place. To the chill-bitten faces of the six men and women who stood above a young man's grave, the birds seemed a word that the wind had spoken.

The Composer

THE MOTHER OF my daughter's best friend called him 'the composer'. She said she bought ironbark honey from him, and that he had a violin for sale. I told her it had to be a good one; Mei was entering Brisbane's Young Conservatorium Orchestra, and I felt it was time she had an instrument befitting the music she would be playing.

'It'll be a good one if he owns it,' she said. 'He's a real composer, you know.'

I asked his name.

'Milo something. Jaarvi. That's it! Milo Jaarvi.'

The name rang a bell, though I did not recall his music. I asked if she knew how much he wanted for the violin. She didn't, but she was sure he would give me a good price.

'He's strange like that,' she said. 'He's honest. He once walked three kilometres to my house after he short-changed me on a tub of honey.'

She gave me an address in the Blackall Range, north of Brisbane.

My daughter was sick that weekend, so I drove out of the city alone. The composer's house was a Queenslander set high in wooded hills near Montville. Peach, olive and citrus trees stood in the front yard. Walking up the stairs I noticed paint peeling from the wallboards. A man of middling height came to the door. His prematurely greying beard and hair made his green eyes startling.

After a brief exchange I was inside with the violin. I have only ever been a mediocre violinist, and the demands of work and family have meant that I can give less and less time to playing. Yet even I could tell the instrument in my hands was exceptional. It was perfectly weighted, and it resonated with such clarity and intensity that I was embarrassed and barely let the bow touch the strings.

'It's a fine fiddle,' I said.

The composer nodded.

'A friend sent it to me from Berlin. It's one hundred and thirty years old. It was almost dead when I got it. I played it back to life over the course of a year. It was made by a Lithuanian out of hundred-year-old Bosnian maple. Biednas was the maker's name. He's barely known, but a true craftsman.'

'I need an instrument for my daughter,' I said. 'But I doubt I can afford this one.'

I told the composer that Mei was going into the Youth Orchestra. Second violin.

'Has she any Jewish blood?'

'My parents are Irish and my wife is Taiwanese. Why do you ask?'

'All the great violinists are Jewish. It's the instrument of the wanderer, the exiled.'

I told him that but for a trip a year to Tainan to visit Mei's grandparents, our family was very much settled.

The composer smiled. He looked out the window at my car on the gravel drive. He asked what work my wife did. I think he was trying to judge my means in order to arrive at a price.

'Twelve thousand,' he said at last.

It was more than I could comfortably afford. But I had

long dreamt that my daughter would become a concert violinist, and she seemed to have aptitude.

I sighed and took out my chequebook.

'No,' said the composer when he saw the cheque. 'Seven thousand five hundred. It's worth much more, but that's what it cost me. Seven thousand five hundred, on the condition that it's for your daughter—that you won't sell it—she must own it for good.'

I thought it was a strange, sentimental request.

'Very well. I promise. Thank you.'

I asked him if he played.

'Not really. Not the violin. I bought it for my own daughter.'

I guessed by the arrangement of the house, its utilitarian furniture and lack of decoration, that the composer lived alone. There was no sign of a woman or child. I did not want to rub the wounds of a broken marriage.

'Daughters.' I smiled consolingly. 'I must have thrown a hundred thousand dollars at Mei's various fads by now. And she's only sixteen.'

The composer nodded and smiled.

I sat down to sign the cheque and took proper stock of the room. A Paling & Co. upright piano stood against the wall, and beside it a handcrafted guitar. Not so much as a painting or photograph adorned the walls. The composer's desk was at the room's one window that looked onto the hills and beyond the hills to the sea. Beside the window stood a small unpolished bookshelf.

I asked the composer if these books were all he had, for I had never known an educated man to possess such a small library. He nodded. I made a mental catalogue of the collection, which was easy as there were only nine volumes: a Greek Bible, *The Brothers Karamazov*, a collection of war stories by Heinrich Böll in the original German, the collected poems of Alfred de Vigny in French, a selection of hymns and writings by St John of Damascus, a book on Arvo Pärt by Paul Hillier, another on music of the early Renaissance, Pseudo-Dionysius's *Mystical Theology* and St. Athanasius's biography of St Anthony.

'Nine books?' I said.

'They keep me going all year. Then I read them again.'

He went to the kitchen to get tea from the stove.

'Forgive me,' I said, 'but are you Catholic, or Orthodox?'

'Neither.' He came back to the table and poured tea. 'Once I belonged to the Greek Orthodox Church.'

'Well, judging by your library, it wasn't reasonable argument that dissuaded you. There are barrel loads of dissuasive books around these days.'

'Yes. Please don't offer me one. It's true I've lost my faith. But an evangelical atheist is no more pleasant or interesting to me than an evangelical Baptist or an evangelical fitness guru. There's enough noise in the world, and I have no time for the kind of people who shout.'

'Forgive me. I had no intention of forcing a book on you. I was curious. You see, my parents were devout Catholics, being Irish, but in recent years I've, well . . . drifted, as they say. I sometimes feel concerned about it, as a family man. I suppose yours is a similar case.'

'No. My break with faith was very sudden.'

'How did it happen?'

'My wife and daughter were killed by a drunk driver.'

I apologised. The composer squinted out the window at the afternoon light.

'My wife was from Berlin. She came to this country with a couple of hundred dollars and her violin. She was busking on La Trobe Terrace when I met her. She was nineteen and very beautiful.' He laughed. 'I wrote a piece for violin and piano in a night, just to get her to stay at my flat to record it. We married shortly after. We lived by the sea, at Shorncliffe. One day after dinner she and our daughter went to buy ice cream. On the walk back home a boy racing a traffic light lost control of his car and hit them at a hundred kilometres an hour.

'Susanne was twenty-seven when she died. My daughter was six. I had believed in God. I had lived through poverty and prejudice, for my faith as well as my art, and believed devoutly . . .' The composer paused and breathed deeply. 'But it was not only the fact of their deaths—as meaningless as it seemed to me—that caused my break with God. That brought me to the brink, but like all Orthodox I expected tragedy of this life. It was compounded absurdity that broke me at last. You see, after they died I set myself to work—it was all I could do to keep going. I resolved to compose a requiem Mass. But I would not hurry it. I composed for ten years. I studied ancient music, even the Hebrew prosody that informed the psalms, which dictated my phrasing. It was a prayer that I prayed for a decade, the only thing of my making that mattered at all. Then, in the very week I finished it, a lazy, barely competent film was released with an even less competent soundtrack that had stolen my themes.'

'Surely not all of them?'

'So many of the important ones . . .but the composer had not understood them. He had not made them mean anything at all, merely tacked them on to the saccharine string passages you find in any other film score. My Mass was unpublished. No conductor would perform it now. God had heard my prayer for ten years. Then He threw it back at me. I thought: How could I have suffered two events so pointless, so deaf, dumb and blind? There was no reason. After that I could not believe.'

I should say that the composer whispered all this. I guessed it was the most he had spoken on the subject in a very long time. He apologised. He was embarrassed. Yet I was curious. I pushed him.

'The theologians say God may be nearest you when you think He's farthest away. And clearly, you're not one of the God-haters.'

'Aren't I?' He shook his head. 'I'm bitter at God for not existing. All the more because the God-shaped dream men have made for Him is so beautiful. You see, I know the theologians are cleverer than the rationalists, that the saints are greater than the materialists, who find this world easy because their imaginations—that cruellest of human faculties—are atrophied. I feel real pain that God has not made Himself exist, if only to justify the finer men. But that is the nature of this world: where rats, diseases and advertising thrive, and tigers, butterflies and poetries die out. It's the vicious, the loud and dull that survive here. The glorious, the lovely, the quiet, the courageous . . .all these must pass away. That is why my wife and child are gone.' The composer lit a cigarette, drew long and flicked the ash into a dirty whisky glass. 'I believe there will come a day, perhaps in your daughter's lifetime, when no man on earth but the paid specialist can hum a bar of Bach's *St Matthew Passion*, when the poetry of de Vigny is not read at all. But perhaps chance will be kind in the future and man's imaginative faculties will evolve away, so he will not feel that loss, nor all the others.'

I was embarrassed by what the composer had said; I was barely aware of de Vigny.

'He was a French poet of the early nineteenth century. "The Wrath of Sampson" is his finest.' The composer closed his eyes to the sunlight and recited a line that resonated with echoes: "'How beautiful will be the feet of the one who comes to announce my death to me.'"

I had the feeling he had recited those words many times before, that they had never lost their melancholy savour. The composer said nothing more until he turned from the window and smiled and apologised again.

Above the books on the composer's shelf was a collection of scores and CD recordings. There were no more than fifty discs. One for each week of the year, he said—though I do not imagine he was really so fastidious or accurate. I noticed some common to my own library: Leonin's *Viderunt Omnes* recorded in the Cathédrale Notre Dame; the Glenn Gould recording of Bach's *Well-Tempered Clavier*; those long improvisations by Vladimir Spivakov on Pärt's *Für Alina* . . . Then I saw a recording of chamber music called *Lux et Nox*; the composer was Milorad Jaarvi.

When I picked up the disc and saw the cover photograph of the dark-haired young man reading a score in the pews of St Stephen's Cathedral, I recognised him at once. I had known him—or known of him—as a first-year student at the Griffith Conservatorium. I dropped out before beginning second year, but I remembered that Milorad Jaarvi, then a postgraduate, was the conservatorium's star. Only the best young musicians were asked to perform his pieces at the biannual concerts.

The recording bore the ABC Classical imprint. On the back I read the release date: 1999.

'Ten years ago. Are there any others?'

'No.'

I wondered out loud: could it be so difficult for a composer with the start he had had to make a career?

'After the death of my family I had no energy left for vanity,' said the composer. 'I could not "push myself", as they say. I rarely send music away nowadays.' He smiled. 'That is not true. I never do.'

'Why do you write if you don't mean your work to be heard?'

'Because I'm a composer. There is nothing else I know to do with the time life gives me. I cannot order the world, so I try to find an order for the silent sounds I mark on pages of staff lines. Though I try very hard to be a farmer instead.'

The composer finished his cigarette and took a folder of manuscript scores from his drawer. He showed me a suite of piano pieces that were built around quotations from Palestrina's *Lamentations of Jeremiah*. The notes were sparely written. Pen strokes and dabs of ink like flecks of birds on a winter sky. I asked him to play one of the pieces. He flattened the score against his leg and sat down at the old upright.

He had excerpted a modal phrase from *Lamentation No.1* that stepped sorrowfully down from its root to arrive at a minor chord, and this he played at varying intervals, in varying rhythms above an accompaniment that at times accepted it, at others resisted, alternating light and dark, home and exile, so the sadness of the motif became exquisite.

'You must publish this!' I said, taking up the rest of the manuscript. 'All of these. They must be performed.'

He smiled and went to his shelf and took up another score, a massive document. At the top of the first page was the title: *Missa ad Susanne et Michelle*, for soprano, alto, tenor and bass.

'It's my requiem Mass. The one I wrote for my little family.'

The pages seemed to have been handled recently.

There was no dust. I touched a quaver on the last page, and the ink remained on my skin.

'You're still writing it. But you said you have no faith.'

The composer sighed.

'I send my prayers into the dark, though I see nothing out there but darkness.'

'Is it finished?' I asked.

'I erase three notes in the morning only to put them back at night.'

He put a compact disc marked with black felt pen on top of the manuscript. The text said *Kyrie/Agnus Dei*.

'The disc contains the first and last movements. I mustered singers from about the district and recorded them in St Finnain's, on Windy Knoll. It's a crude recording, but you can take it if you want. I have copies.'

'Come with me,' I said. 'We'll find a copier for the score. It's just possible I can get this performed.'

'Take the manuscript.'

'What if I lose it? It could be a masterpiece.'

The composer smiled, almost laughed, as if he had not heard the word in many years. I realised that the music before me had nothing to do with ambition.

The sunlight had vanished into the hills. A wind rose in the east over the ocean, blowing the curtains and making the composer's room cold.

I finished my tea and took up the violin along with the score and recording.

'I should go,' I said. 'My family will be waiting.'

'Of course.'

I took my car down the gravel road and onto the asphalt. I slipped the disc into the player and heard the voices of four amateur singers carrying a Mass inside a tiny wooden church. After a few moments of listening, the wind in the microphone, the shuffling of feet and the creaking of floorboards seemed to vanish. The Mass left the building and floated in the darkening foothills of the range. I recognised the notes of the film score Jaarvi had mentioned, but the phrasing and then the deep structure I began to perceive changed the notes utterly, till the film score faded into oblivion and I knew that if I ever heard it again it would only seem to me a faint, fragmented echo of a voice that had spoken to me clearly this night. The road swung out onto a ledge that revealed the last flush of blue dusk over the ocean. I pulled the car off to the side and listened to the *Agnus Dei*, to all the beautiful anguish the composer had poured into the God-shaped hole that resided in his heart. We will all lose everything, I thought. And perhaps then, by the very shape of our pain, we may earn it back. A solitary soprano note swept across the face of the water toward an infinite horizon.

The Source of the Silence

When my soul is bathed in light that is not bound by space;
when it listens to sound that never dies away . . .
—St Augustine, Confessions, Book 10.6

A CALENDAR ON THE motel room's wall tells me
fifteen years have passed. I had a sister who was
fourteen then and has never grown older. I turn from
the window and the commercial street where neon-lit
advertisements press their inanities upon the night, and
I recall the half-dozen of her spoken phrases that I still
possess, and I remember her sleeping in a room where
I stood awake; the touch of her hand in the dark. So
much more I have lost to this world of gathering noise. I
wonder what can be retrieved, though I will not retrieve
or lose much more. A year ago I was diagnosed with a
rare heart condition. I will not explain it, because it bores
me. Suffice to say that any year, any day my losses may
cease . . .

We lived in the Brisbane Valley, that unthought-of
tract of land an hour west of the city. There were more
cold nights than warm; kangaroo and red deer stood
side by side in the mist-shrouded woods I hunted with a
break-action shotgun and a box of rifled slug shells; and
the expansive, breathing emptiness of plain, highway and
hills was the universe and not somewhere on the outskirts of it. Today the place grows steadily into an undis-

tinguished outer-suburb of both Brisbane and Ipswich, which sprawling cities care nothing for it and will shortly lose it forever. But back then we were isolated. We were very poor and very happy and not aware of either. We did not know the world's meanest habits. And in the twilight of my childhood, I could hear words my sister had not yet spoken.

The words were neither auditory nor imaginary. I was as certain of the ability as I was of my ability to breathe. I remember one instance clearly. Irene slept in my room when our father left late at night for where she did not know and I would not tell her. I was staring out my bedroom window onto the plains. The words, *you must always look after me* came like pencils of light from the immense emptiness. And then she spoke them. I patted down her dark hair and smiled and returned my eyes to the plain. Nothing seemed extraordinary back then and with her, or perhaps I should say that everything did, so her silent words were not rarer flowers to me than the words she spoke aloud.

As children we were very wild and very religious. The two states seemed perfectly harmonious. Religion was a thousands-of-years old Eastern book, and icons of fierce-eyed long-bearded or serenely feminine, miracle working saints. Our mother died of post partum haemorrhage giving birth to the daughter who took her name, and the only adult guidance we had came in the form of an aging Ursuline nun, a tireless domestic worker and devout mystic. Once a week Sister Maria Nivard would come to our house to make sure we were fed and clean. She would bake us a simple cake, or bring bread and canned fish and soap. Despite all her learning and the hardships of religious life she was as meek as a kitten and was careful to avoid our father, who mocked her 'superstitions'—'A religion for worms that takes life from a corpse,' he quoted in front of her. Then she sighed and her fading blue eyes seemed to be staring at something far away.

But when she had us alone she told us the kinds of stories our teachers and father could never tell: of missionary work in India, of the incorrupt bodies of St Cecilia and St Bernadette Soubirous, and the propositions of St Augustine, which she had a knack for making simple. In the language of children we contemplated time, light, darkness and the spaceless substance of angels.

Sister Nivard told me the universe was made after the principles of music. On my mother's neglected piano she held down middle C and played an E to show how the first note sounded sympathetically, to prove harmony was secreted in nature and not merely a construct of the mind. And she revealed the mystery of melody: that we may transpose it into the various modes so all the notes are changed; quicken or slow the tempo; hear it through a man-made instrument as well as sung . . . so in the end we have something that in physical substance has nothing in common with the original. Yet we recognise it. We recognise it anywhere . . . 'Even if a count lasts a second or a year.'

I asked if the pattern would not be lost if a note was sustained for a year.

I believe I thought of my mother when I asked that question.

'Not if we were pure and patient of mind. It would not be lost to God, who sees all time as we see a picture.'

We turned from the piano. Irene was asleep on the bare floorboards in the sunlight that poured through the living room window. Her hair was black and her face, always, ghostly pale. Some women of the town thought she looked sick. She was not sick, though in infancy she had both anaemia and whooping cough and might have died at any hour. It almost hurt to look upon her, so deli-cately formed and apparently unfit for the world.

Sister Nivard smiled: 'Isn't she beautiful.'

I nodded.

'Do any of the local boys think so?'

'No,' I said sharply, a little shocked at the question that had never occurred to me.

Sister Nivard explained inherited guilt and the inevi-tability of sin. My sins were so great I prayed kneeling by my bed, sometimes from nine until midnight, watching a candle that burnt my eyes until I saw sparks.

Like everyone, I have seen the euphoric television ministries; like everyone in the Arts faculty at the univer-sity where I spent half a year of my early twenties I was a nominal socialist. I begrudged the Church for chaining a boy to his bedside for guilt, the guilt I would not lose now for all the world; the guilt I indulge this night I sit lonely at my window, remembering a girl — a workmate at a bottle shop — with whom I spent evenings such as this three years ago. One afternoon she and I walked along Ithaca Creek in the city's northwest. She pushed her dark hair from her eyes and told me one day soon she would like to get married.

I nodded.

'Irene,' I whispered by accident when at dusk I found a feather-tailed gliders nest in a grey gum. I was a way behind her on the track. I watched to see if she heard. If she would turn.

I am separated from that girl tonight by only a few physical miles, a telephone call rather than the ocean of death, yet I do not go to her. Perhaps she is already married and would not welcome me. There are many kinds of distance. How strange I would feel arriving on her doorstep . . .

That summer the town's neglected boys and I would walk down to Mary Smokes Creek to keep a vigil we did not understand. We lit fires at the edge of the woods and watched sparks fly into the cold night air and stars singe the edge of the plain. We scattered the fires with our boots and walked in the dark in fields that were not ours, yet we claimed them, as the last ones awake when the dark seemed to enfeeble all Man's claims.

One night I left the boys early. Something told me Irene was not sleeping, that she would not till I returned. Not many weeks later she would be killed by a man who could not bear her beauty, a man who packed groceries at a shopping centre fifty kilometres east on the highway — I put a shotgun slug an inch above his heart before he escaped in his truck onto Highway 54. But this night my sister was still close enough to touch . . .

I kicked off my boots and came into her room and whatever anxiety my truancy had caused vanished from her face. She did not care that I was late, only that finally I had come. She kissed the lamp-lit hands of the Black Madonna of Częstochowa and brushed her hair from her eyes: as though I were in any danger in that landscape I knew so well.

She asked me if we could go to the back steps and watch the stars. Tip-toeing and whispering along the creaking corridor meant the laws of the house were recognised, they were only being respectfully disobeyed. So even if our father was home and heard us, we knew he would not rise.

From those splintered steps we watched the night. We sat in silence punctuated by the wind that blew waves through the long grass and sang in the plainwire of a paddock fence. Irene turned her eyes to the firmament while I watched the inconstant terrestrial lights. I could not name the constellations as she did. Since birth my right eye has been amblyopic and cannot bring anything into focus, and at twelve my left eye began to fail. So I wondered what made the lower lights and why. I brought Irene into my game. We imagined a wandering torch searched for some unjustified runaway child; red brake-lights on a back road indicated a young man's tragic path to a card game or conspiratorial meeting of horse thieves; a far distant orange glow was lovers kissing by lantern light . . . Finally I watched the plain for the simple wonder of narrow light upon an immense darkness. I imagined that the lights of farmhouses and distant highway lamps had no physical source, that they were manifest for no other reason than to divide the dark.

Was it directly then, after admitting my dream of the lights, that I heard her silent voice: 'Follow me, I know the way home.'

I laughed.

'I thought we were home?' I spoke aloud.

She furrowed her brow.

An ephemeral creek cut my father's land and disap-peared into the wood to the north. Irene pointed to it and took my hand. We climbed through the barbwire fence at the back of the yard and walked to the water, to that reach of the creek where cedar and river she oak hugged the bank. We came out of the trees, to a gouge six feet wide in the grass, where the water and the Milky Way ran a parallel course. Irene looked across the plain. She laughed. Whatever place she had been leading me was not here, though perhaps this resembled it; echoed it. She looked to the stars with questioning eyes, as though her silent words had come from there. I too looked up and felt there was a pattern, like music or poetry, but a pattern too deep, too broad and patient to discover in a lifetime let alone a night. Irene looked now to the heavens, now across the earth. 'This is wrong,' she said. 'Just slightly wrong. But God remembers how it should be.' Then she sighed and smiled so her eyes were crescents. I looked into her eyes and, like her words that led me, like the starlight that reached us here, near and distant at once, I would leave my body behind if I might.

She took my hand again.

'Let's go back.'

An hour ago a young woman called and told me not to come to her house if it became too late, if I was tired. She is a tutor at the theological college where I have worked maintaining motor vehicles for the past year. I told her I would see her tomorrow; that we would walk in the woods again in the afternoon, or perhaps drive into the western hills to some tracks I walk alone and often. The tracks branch off the road through the cedar hills and the road goes to the place I grew up, but I do not ever drive so far. In July I walked the cooling forest with her; I watched her tie her dark hair, to see if she might tie it so it so it bunched and rested on her right shoulder; and I wondered if she might recognise some track or other, some tree: the old Watkins Fig whose cavernous roots a dark-haired, runaway child had slept in all those years ago.

I suspect this woman is already tiring of my strange ways, the solitude and pensiveness that have been called poetic temperament by my few friends, but in that unlikely 'later' I might yet live to see, will make me merely a strange old man. "Loneliness made him like that," people will say. And they will be right; and they will be wrong.

She wished me goodnight over a crystal clear telephone line. I did not answer. She laughed and complained I was not listening to her. But I was listening, to the timbre of her voice, and to the fading light in the eucalypts and cedars falling through all the lost afternoons of childhood; and I was listening to the night when a policeman came to the stairs and told me the most terrible thing I will ever hear and I fell to my knees and prayed to God to bring her back to me, though it was against his law and will, and I would suffer anything rather than be without her. I was given hope by the strange events that followed her: her unlikely survival of infancy and the words she could place inside my mind, as though they existed without the world.

And now, fifteen years and a world away in an outskirts motel room, I was listening, as ever, for words my soul so longs to hear again: the words that led me one night to a place that was almost the place she meant. *Follow me, I know the way home.*

I have sat many times at the windows of temporary homes such as this one, longing for that place . . . But there are times that I cannot reclaim her face. I still possess the sound of her voice, but even that is leaving me. And I wonder if I have ceased to believe in her. Is my sitting by the window and the dark now, thoughts turned to the dark-haired pale-skinned girl who called me tonight, asleep in a suburban house only a train ride away, an act of faith or despair?

I sat awake with a bottle of whisky. I sat long awake with a bottle of whisky and heard the last train of the night arrive and depart.

I felt the familiar pain in my chest, the pins and needles in my feet that meant I should walk. I stepped out into the courtyard. The crisp night air took my breath. The motel gardener had stayed late. He stopped and stared.

'You alright, Patrick?'

'Nothing I can't walk off.'

I was alone at the edge of the courtyard. I do not know how long I stood and stared at the stars. I forgot about the pain, forgot about my breath. The constellations and coloured giants were as vivid as flames jumping at the ends of tapers. A dark-haired girl walked off the asphalt and between buildings. Only the starlight lit her face. I smiled.

'I didn't think you'd come.'

She pressed my hand and turned me along the path. I huddled close to her shoulder.

'Where are we going?'

Acknowledgements

'Flame Bugs on the Sixth Island' first appeared in *The Griffith Review: How Nigh's the End*, No.12, 2006.

'Integrity' first appeared in *Wet Ink*, No. 13, Summer 2008/2009.

'A Haunted Solitude' first appeared in *Etchings*, No.6, Summer 2008/2009.

'The Passenger' first appeared in *Wet Ink*, No. 9, Summer 2007/2008.

'The Sons of Cain' was runner up in the 2007 Fish Short Histories Competition, and first appeared in *Mississippi River Blues: Fish Anthology 2008*.

'The City Lost to Heaven' first appeared in *The Griffith Review: In the Neighbourhood*, No. 18, November 2007.

'In the City of Exiles' is the runner-up in the 2009 E J Brady Short Story Competition.

'By the Aral Sea' first appeared in *Wet Ink*, No. 13, Summer 2008/2009.

'Music for Airports' first appeared in *Best Australian Stories 2008,* Black Inc. November 2008.

'The Composer' first appeared in *The Griffith Review,* 'Stories for Today', No 26, November 2009 .

'The Source of the Sound' first appeared in *Quadrant*, Volume LII Number 451, November 2008.

Special thanks to my family and everyone at Salt.

PATRICK HOLLAND grew up in outback Queensland, where he worked as a horseman before moving to Brisbane. His is the author of two novels: *The Long Road of the Junkmailer* (UQP, 2006), which won the Queensland Premier's Award for Best Emerging Author and was shortlisted for the Commonwealth Writer's Prize, Best First Book, and *The Mary Smokes Boys* (Transit Lounge, 2010). *The Source of the Sound* is his debut story collection and a winner of the inaugural Scott Prize. A collection of his travel essays, *Riding the Trains in Japan*, will appear in 2011.